MARKED FOR MURDER

'Leave this affair alone, Martinson — Jean Hallison is dead . . . !' The caller had rung off, leaving Inspector Jim Martinson wondering if this was a bluff. Had Jean been murdered? And where did the suave, grinning Montoni fit in? He was accused of assaulting two women — but at the same time Jim himself had been watching him elsewhere. Now, however, Jim links the chain of evidence — slowly tightening the rope that will bring in the sinister gang that is terrorising Framcastle.

NORMAN LAZENBY

MARKED FOR MURDER

Complete and Unabridged

LINFORD
Leicester

First published in Great Britain

First Linford Edition
published 2011

British Library CIP Data

Lazenby, Norman A. (Norman Austin)
 Marked for murder. - -
 (Linford mystery library)
 1. Detective and mystery stories.
 2. Large type books.
 I. Title II. Series
 813.5'4–dc22

 ISBN 978–1–4448–0898–8

Published by
F. A. Thorpe (Publishing)
Anstey, Leicestershire

Set by Words & Graphics Ltd.
Anstey, Leicestershire
Printed and bound in Great Britain by
T. J. International Ltd., Padstow, Cornwall

This book is printed on acid-free paper

Marked for Murder

1

The Unknown Menace

When Detective-Inspector Jim Martinson walked into the Palais de Danse he expected to see some queer fellows, but because he was officially off duty he intended to regard them with an indulgent eye. He had wondered into the huge danceland because the night was his own and he thought a spot of dancing was a good idea.

Jim Martinson forgot that being off duty was an impossible state of mind to him, and had been nearly all the eleven years of his service in Framcastle City Police. He was the youngest detective-inspector the detective branch had had to suffer in all its turbulent years of existence.

For Framcastle, a big ugly sprawling city, lay along the banks of a muddy industrial river, and many were the odd events that happened among the labyrinth of riverside streets and warehouses. These brawls, fires, raids, alarms and sudden deaths were ugly but exciting, and to many clever gentlemen who lived in more sedate streets, they were often profitable incidents.

Jim Martinson had tasted these ingredients and emerged unscathed. The life, all in all, he decided, was not too bad.

Especially when one had the run of a department and an unusual amount of freedom and a superior like Superintendent Barlow. The Super had been like a father to him.

Jim took his huge frame into the hall, and many were the immediate glances from flushed, excitable girls. He was a big man in every way. Men like Jim Martinson, are, in point of fact, met only rarely, for his size instantly caused the ordinary man to look up and enviously compare measurements. Yet he was not simply a towering hulk, for his hands, though capable, had a suggestion of fineness in their strength. And there was intelligence behind those grey eyes and geniality in his firm mouth

Immediately he bumped into one of the odd fellows it was his business to know. The man was slim-waisted and his black hair was shining like patent leather. It made a great contrast to Jim Martinson's sandy, crisp locks.

'Hello, Lem.' murmured Jim. 'Fancy meeting you here.'

He received an unpleasant stare from Lemuel Dallas as the man strolled away.

Jim lit a cigarette and idly followed the man's progress. Lem moved like a cat. Some might have said instantly that the man was a ridiculous lounge lizard, but Jim Martinson knew better.

'Strange how one is always meeting one's pet aversion,' muttered Jim.

Then he grinned cheerfully. He looked round for a really tall girl and within ten seconds he was dancing with her and commencing to be conversational.

The Palais de Dance at Framcastle is a huge gilded hall and two bands play in succession to each other so that there need not be any lengthy pause between dances. The two bands, sitting in their terraced alcove sometimes play together and then the scream of saxophones and the beat of drums is almost sufficient to lift the roof. The roof, however, resists the vibrations on nearly all occasions, even when the sprung floor is bouncing strongly,

No one cares, and quite rightly. The patrons have paid to make merry and nothing else matters. Excitable laughter, snatches of song and the loud hum of conversation from the people sitting at the tables, are testimony to the thrilling atmosphere. That there is an element of vice mixing with the innocent pleasure-seekers is only the business of men like Detective-Inspector Jim Martinson.

More than once his grey eyes lost their gleam and became speculative as he saw an undoubtedly shady character gliding round with an apparent victim. But it was the girl who was dancing with Lem Dallas who caused Jim's eyes to stare.

She was glamorous, her hair was red and she was clad in a daring pale green dress. Jim manoeuvred closer with his partner. The redhead was certainly vivacious, like most of her type. She was laughing carelessly, her head thrown back and her warm, red lips parted. On closer inspection, Jim decided she was not his type, but he was still interested. Anyone who danced with Lem and liked it was interesting.

He smiled thinly. Not even the most sophisticated girl would consider dancing with Lem if they knew his true profession. And those who came willingly to meet him did not want to dance.

The music sobbed to a finish, and there was just time to escort his partner off the floor and glance round for Lem Dallas when the indicator stated that the next dance would be a quickstep.

Jim wasted no time. He slipped over to where Lem and the redhead stood, and at that moment the two bands crashed into a nonstop rhythmic number. Jim cut in between Lem and the girl with a coolness that was bred of absolute confidence in his ability to carry off any stunt. He saw a snarl flick Lem's lips; but Jim Martinson was smiling down at the redhead.

In seconds they were gliding over the

floor. He had given her no time for a refusal, and she wasn't quite sure how it came she was dancing — so divinely — with this light-haired young giant.

He smiled down. 'Thanks for dancing. I'd made up my mind you wouldn't turn me down.'

She wasn't tall, but he had the knack of dancing with girls of average height. 'You make refusal hard, big boy,' she said. 'I was going to dance with someone else.'

'I know — Lem.'

'He'll be mad. But Lem is not a bad sort. So you know him?'

'Like a brother. I have to keep my eye on him.'

She gave him a sharp glance. 'I don't think Lem allows anyone to keep an eye on him. What do you mean, big boy?'

'Look,' said Jim calmly, 'I'm Detective-Inspector Jim Martinson, of the City Police. Lem is a rat — that's too mild, but you're a lady.' Jim nearly said: 'I hope,' under his breath. 'Let me tell you something — go away and never see Lem Dallas again. Keep away — unless you know all about him.'

8

She was quick to snap back. 'What do you mean — know all about him?'

He looked into those brown eyes curiously. 'Lem Dallas is in the world's worst racket. He deals in women. He's an agent for some unholy swine who controls a vice ring up and down the river. Who is the big man? That's something we'd like to know. Why don't we pull in Lem? Well, he's been 'in' before, and I'll get him again with the greatest of pleasure someday, just when I've got the evidence nicely totalled up. Now do you know all that Red?'

To conclude his words, he swung her in an elaborate turn.

'Aren't you clever!' she said. 'Of course, I guessed a lot about Mr. Lem, and I can take care of myself, thank you, Detective. If it is worrying you, I can say. Lem will never get me.'

'The man he works for doesn't always ask your permission before he snatches you into his ring.'

'Thanks for the concern, but I'm all right. Lem and I are great pals.'

'Okay, Red.' Jim gave her a wicked

smile. 'I've done my best.'

'My name is Jean Hallison,' she said, and she pressed closer.

Jim grinned down into two impish eyes. She was pretty even if she was over-painted.

'And you know mine,' he said. 'Ring me up at Police Headquarters when you need rescuing.'

'You could ring me up even though I don't need rescuing.'

'And the number?'

'Central 2217. Don't grin so much, or Lem will guess. Steer over there. If you're slightly interested in the address it's Moor Park Flats. Number Two — on the top floor. I share a tiny flat with Linda.'

Jim Martinson was secretly amused at her bold efforts to secure his interest, yet he promptly asked: 'Who is Linda?' One of the reasons for his meteoric promotion was the results he achieved through asking plenty of questions. Jim was never loth to ask a question.

'Linda's my friend. She's awfully good — I don't know why she sticks by me. I mean — I try her pretty heavily and we don't go the same places and we don't always meet the same people.'

'She wouldn't like Lem, eh?'

'Did you have to say that?' snapped Jean Hallison. 'No, she doesn't know about Lem. But she's not stuffy, thank God. Linda can put on her sophistication with the best of them.'

'I'll call and take you both out,' said Jim rapidly.

'Thanks — but I left school years ago.'

'Not so many years surely,' he said gently.

She was looking into his face without a sign of wavering. It was a provocative look, he knew.

'About Linda,' he persisted. 'Don't you two work somewhere?'

'Sure. Linda works. She got a steady job as a secretary for a big business man. I dodged away from work as soon as I saw a way to get past the restrictions. I want to be a singer.'

'Do you sing for your supper, rent and clothes?'

She stared hard at him. 'Listen. I shouldn't like your nerve. You don't care what you say to a girl. If you want to know — I've got some money. It was left me a little while ago.'

He nodded his head gravely. 'Lucky you. Once I was left a 1918 model car, and it didn't work. So you're not actually working as a singer?'

'No. I practice and take lessons. Good heavens — what a bore the woman who teaches me is! I'm sick of her.'

'Are you good? I mean — can you sing well? I guess Linda thinks you are, eh?'

'Linda is like a sister, I tell you. Years ago we came from the same district and that's why we stick together. And if I had a mike, I'd show you whether I'm good.'

'You can be good to me, and my name's not Mike,' murmured Jim.

She gave a sigh of exasperation, and then the bands finally came to the end of their piece in a frenzy of brass and drums.

'That's -a-all!' sang out the slick band leader, and Jim escorted the redhead back to the scowling Lem Dallas.

Jim Martinson had methodically filed all the information he'd got from Jean

Hallison, and it was tucked away in a recess of his mind. It seemed trivial enough — the chatter of a shallow girl. But she was playing with fire, running round with the smooth Lem Dallas and if anything went wrong and the affair came into his province, he'd at least know something about the girl.

Little did he realise then that the grim shadow of Fate was about to play a card.

After a couple of dances with two girls who began to be gushing as soon as he smiled at them, he found himself wishing he was back in his office, or alternatively, having a drink with Ted Delaney. Delaney was a chubby young man with a more than usual capacity for drink — mostly beer — and he knew all the public houses in Framcastle. Ted cherished ambitions to become a private detective in spite of the fact that a private detective in England has not the official status that he has in the United States. Ted Delaney had missed the bus, in his early years, in not joining the City Police; but he was not unduly worried. He was owner of a thriving motor car sales depot. Next to beer his chief interest lay in driving a powerful car.

No one had ever seen him combine the two hobbies. Ted at a wheel was a steady, keen-eyed individual.

Yes, he should have looked up Ted and not gone looking for stinkers in this paradise of pick-ups and psuedo gentlemen.

Two dances jazzed by and then Jim noticed the green-suited bandleader stand before the mike. An announcement, decided the detective.

'Will a Miss Jean Hallison proceed to the foyer, please? A Miss Jean Hallison, wanted outside. Very important. Thank you.'

Jim Martinson did not waste time discrediting his ears. The announcement was clear enough. The laws of sheer chance operating again, he thought. Or was it? He felt curious.

He saw Jean dashing to her cloakroom, and she had left Lem Dallas.

Jim strolled up to the man. 'No serious news for our little Jean, I trust? No one ill, or anything?'

'She didn't tell me anything,' said Lem thinly. 'An' it's no business of yours.' Lem's black eyes spat hatred. A white handkerchief lolled ridiculously from his breast pocket.

'Everybody's business is mine,' murmured Jim Martinson. 'Who is waiting for Jean in the foyer?'

'How should I know?'

'Aren't you going to accompany the lady in case she needs assistance?'

Lem glared, while he fastened the buttons of his tight-fitting double-breasted jacket. 'You must waste a lot of time asking fool questions, Martinson!'

'All in the interests of justice,' said Jim virtuously. 'Well, here's the lady herself!'

And Jean Hallison came running up. She had put on a thick camel hair coat, and she was tying the belt. Her hair was covered by a gay scarf. She looked, Jim admitted, an intriguing piece of work even though her tongue was as sharp as a dagger.

She nodded archly to Jim, and stopped to speak breathlessly to Lem. 'See you tomorrow, Lem. Same place, same time.' She smiled at Jim Martinson. 'Good night, big boy.'

'What's the trouble? Why have you got to go?' queried Martinson.

'Linda's ill. That's what they've told me. The doctor attending her has sent his car here to pick me up.'

'Was she ill when you left her?'

Jean Hallison gazed at him uncertainly. 'Didn't seem to be, now that you mention it. I expect it is something sudden. Heaven knows what the doctor expects me to do — I hate sick people. But it'll be awful if I don't hurry along — I mean I've got to go now.'

'Yes, not much else, is there?' rejoined Jim dryly.

He noticed Lem Dallas had made no suggestion about escorting the girl or travelling with her in case extra help was needed. But of course it was useless to expect the ordinary decencies of conduct from Lem. The man was utterly callous, self-seeking and he considered purely the profit or convenience of any situation. Lem would not help a drowning man if it

16

required wetting his shoes.

'Would you like me to go along with you — might need a man!' said Jim in a joking tone.

Jean Hallison was half-turned away and she glanced back.

'Good God — a sick room is no place to bring a guest. Some other time. I've got to be going.'

She walked quickly through the babbling, laughing groups of pleasure-makers, reached the door leading to the foyer

'Hope you can see Jean doesn't want anyone to tag along with her, said Lem in a venomous voice. 'An' keep your nose out of my private life, Martinson, or — '

'Or what?' Jim's words were soft. 'Don't talk to me like that, you third-rate little mess! I might make you eat those words — dipped in poison!'

But Lem Dallas turned away. The fury in his face did not alarm Martinson.

The big man turned and walked to the foyer door. Something — was it the fact that Linda's illness was extraordinarily sudden, or Lem's disinclination to accompany Jean Hallison? — something irked his mind. Something told him to follow Jean a little further.

He came down the foyer steps with increasing speed. It was an almost deserted place. A few young men were sitting on secluded settees, waiting for their friends. A burly commissionaire stood at the top of the steps, and he nodded to Jim Martinson. But Jim only returned the nod. He did not stop. He could not see Jean Hallison.

The strident strains of the bands floated to his ears. As incidental music it was incongruous in this quiet setting where the cold street air circulated. Jim came to the street door and looked round.

He was just in time to see a small blue car with the driver climbing quickly into his seat. A street lamp shone its pale rays into the car's interior, and Jim caught a glimpse of Jean Hallison's face as she sat back in the rear seat.

He strode rapidly across the pavement. His walk ended in an impulsive leap, but he was a fraction too late. The driver had shot out his clutch. The car tore away with protesting engine and a crashing of gears.

Jim swore. He'd wanted a look at that driver. He'd got an uneasy feeling about the S.O.S. call to Jean Hallison. He had felt that way from the beginning. There was something not quite right — yes, he had it! He'd have been happier if there had been verification of the authenticity of that S.O.S.

And the car driver had started off as if the hounds of hell were on his tail. Or had the appearance of a big man coming forward with every indication of interference startled him?

Jim Martinson thought it had. And he knew what he had to do. He bounded up the steps. A few seconds later he burst into the danceland manager's office. That ornament was not present, but a little clerk, with childish blue eyes, blinked while Jim grabbed the telephone and jerked out explanations.

He got straight through to Detective-Sergeant Stan Burrell, whom he knew would be on duty and whom he could rely on to act promptly. Burrell was in charge of a number of police patrol cars.

'Stan, have a car come round at once to the Palais de Danse, pick me up. I've got a call to make. And I know it's damned little to go on, but there is such a thing as luck and I want a blue saloon, which has just left the Palais, traced if possible. The car shot along Wordsworth Avenue. Anyway, get the patrols to look for a blue saloon, two or three year old. Number? Hell, I couldn't see it! I'll call you again — be able to tell you if the whole thing's a false alarm.'

The police car arrived within minutes. Jim jumped in.

'We're going to Moor Park Flats,' he said.

If Jean Hallison was at home, his hunch had been screwy. If she was not — but he'd soon know. After all, anything could happen to that redhead. She was playing with fire.

Moor Park Flats were a modem edifice of the tiny service flatlet type. A large garage housed many cars, but Jim did not bother to look for the blue saloon. He went quickly to the lift and was shot up to the top floor. The lift-girl showed him to Number Two.

He pressed a bell in the imitation rosewood wall.

Presently the door opened and framed in the space was a tall girl. She was really tall and yet graceful with an alert figure. Cool grey eyes looked inquiringly into his.

'You are Linda,' said Martinson. 'Please excuse me, but — has Jean Hallison arrived home?'

'Jean is at some dance,' said Linda.

'And you are not ill?' It was a statement, more than a question.

'Heavens, no! Why should I be? Are you?'

Jim let out a deep breath. 'No. I see you don't understand. Have you got a 'phone?'

'Certainly. And there's one in the hall. Are you one of Jean's boy friends?'

Her voice was cool, intelligent. Martinson did not need more than a second to appraise her. Here was breeding — a rare indefinable quality in sharp contrast to the redhead's blatant airs. Linda's hair was dark, and there was a certain look of sophistication in her high Pompadour coiffure. She was wearing a simple but expensively cut skirt and blouse.

'I'm not Jean's or anyone else's boy friend,' said Jim. 'I'm a detective officer — Detective-Inspector Jim Martinson. I have a confounded card somewhere. I — er — ' Jim looked squarely at her. 'I have every reason to believe that Miss Hallison has been kidnapped or perhaps worse.'

She was resourceful.

'Perhaps you'd better use my 'phone, Inspector.'

He entered the flat, went immediately to the instrument.

'That you, Stan?' he said eventually. 'Martinson speaking. 'Fraid that the Hallison girl has been kidnapped. She is not at her home, and that proves that the S.O.S. was a fake.'

Burrell's metallic voice said: 'The patrols are looking for the saloon, but there isn't much to work on,'

Jim replaced the receiver.

'I don't like it,' he said. 'I met your friend, Jean, at a dance-hall and she told me a few things that made me realise she was playing some foolish game. Then came an S.O.S.'

And Jim Martinson went on to tell the girl all that had transpired. He did not rush through the recital, for he found he was reluctant to terminate this meeting with the tall girl.

'And that's all I know,' he finished. 'Unless you can add to my information, Miss Linda?'

'Linda Davies,' she supplied, and then she was thoughtful. She was presently about to speak when the telephone rang.

'That'll be Stan Burrell,' said Martinson.

But it was not Burrell's homely accents that came to his ears.

'Am I speaking to Inspector Martinson? Ah, I thought you would be there. Better leave this affair alone, Martinson. Give it to someone else.' The voice was cultured and threatening, Jim knew. 'Jean Hallison is dead. You'll find her eventually. She was very silly — unfortunately I can tell you no more. And there are others like Jean.

Good night, Inspector.' And the voice ended with a chuckle.

Grimly Martinson called the exchange. 'I want that call traced if possible.' And he gave his name.

'Only Lem and the Police knew I was coming to this flat,' he muttered. 'Only Lem and the police.'

2

Another Attack

He looked steadily at Linda Davies, noted the pucker of curiosity on her forehead. He walked a pace or two and then turned to face her.

'Miss Davies — that call was from some mysterious devil and he told me that Jean Hallison is dead.'

She stared. Then she sank to a seat very slowly

Jim said: 'Can I get you something to drink?' For once he felt acutely embarrassed in contact with a girl. He came closer, put a hand on her shoulder. 'I'm afraid I couldn't put it more tactfully. I'm afraid I'm rather a bull at times.'

She was undoubtedly shaken. With admiration he realised she was not going to indulge in hysterics or false emotional storms. That was just as well, for he could only be cynical in the face of that type,

'I suppose — it — is — murder. It can't be anything else. Poor Jean! Oh, poor Jean! I should have kept her away from her so-called friends.'

'She was rather wilful?' suggested Jim.

'Oh — I know she was foolish at times — but — oh, murder! Why? It is horrible! What has she done?'

'I could easily imagine another form of disaster coming to her after the things she told me,' said Martinson. 'I did not expect murder.'

'Who was the man who called you?'

'I'd give an awful lot to learn that,' returned Jim grimly. 'Judging from his voice, he's one of these clever birds whose biggest fault is that he has to scrape some satisfaction out of his exploits. He did not have to 'phone me. I'll make a little prophecy, Linda. We'll get that clever boy through that failing.'

The next few minutes were occupied with the telephone exchange. The call from the mysterious speaker had gone out from a street callbox. It was just as Martinson had expected. He rang through to Police Headquarters, called Detective-Sergeant Burrell.

'The girl is dead, Stan. Murdered. Put out a general call. The killer says we'll find the girl eventually. Didn't say where. He likes to play games but he isn't very sporting — kinda meagre with the dues. He called me from a street booth, from the West End area. You can act on that. I'll be over soon as I can.'

Martinson swung to Linda Davies, his long legs astride a velveteen easy chair arm.

'The killer mentioned that there are others like Jean. I wonder what that means. Did Jean know many girls — I mean in a special way?'

'She knew heaps.' Linda turned to the 'phone, commenced to ring down for some tea to be sent up from the kitchens. 'I'm afraid I feel the need for tea, Inspector. How about you, while I tell you all I can about Jean and her friends?'

'Thanks. And — er — ' he had to smile — 'don't call me 'Inspector'. No one does, not even the blokes who are supposed to stand in awe of me. I'm Jim

Martinson to most people.'

He was glad she smiled.

'Okay, Mr. Martinson. You'll have to ask a lot of questions, won't you? No doubt before you find the — the horrible fiend who killed Jean, I'll get to the 'Jim' stage.'

'I hope so. Jean had a lot of friends? Now to save time, could you outline any who are in any way disreputable or likely to have any connection with murder? And her enemies — if she had any — do you know them?'

A maid brought in some tea and presently Martinson was balancing a delicate cup and saucer in one hand.

'I wonder why Jean Hallison was killed?' Jim said speculatively. 'Find the motive here and we're halfway to the killer.'

'I think the man you call Lem might point a way to a motive. I have never met him, and I suppose he's a sample of some of Jean's 'friends'. There might be dozens like him, for all I know.' Linda held her cup thoughtfully.

'We'll pick up Lem before the morning,' said Martinson. 'As to the actual murder; I think he has an alibi. Though I'm certain he *knew*, though that's no proof. But I'm interested in Jean's girl friends. You see, I want to prevent another murder.'

Linda's long-lashed eyes were very serious. 'Apart from myself, Jean had two other special friends. They were all girls who liked a good time.' Linda smiled. 'That meant they liked hectic pleasures, noisy orchestras and noisy men. I'm sure there was no harm in their exploits. Surely you don't believe their lives are in danger?'

'The killer hinted that there were others like Jean. I wish he had been more specific.' Martinson did not worry easily, but a furrow appeared on his brow. 'Now the names and addresses of these two girls?'

'June Carlow — she's blonde and clever. And Elsa Mawn. She is not so clever and not quite so blonde as June. They both live together in a tiny house and fend for themselves. They are a duet at Montoni's club in Fenn Street. They ought to be doing their stuff now, and I'm not so sure they'll go straight home. Their address is 10 Oval Drive, Highbourne.'

'Jean had ambitions to sing. Did she ever get the chance?'

'I'm afraid she lacked just that something,' said Linda quietly. 'Though she was improving. I couldn't persuade her to take an ordinary job ever since she was left that money.'

Martinson stood up. For a moment she looked appreciatively at his height, and he caught the look. They both laughed simultaneously.

'Yes, I make tailors groan. However — was Jean left much?'

'She really never told me. But Jean could pay her bills and that requires real money. She evidently had it.'

Martinson put out a hand for the telephone. He dialled and soon began speaking to Burrell at Police Headquarters. 'I'm going over to Montoni's Club, Stan. Incidentally, better pick up Lem Dallas, last seen inside the Palais de Danse. I'm fairly sure he knows something about the girl's murder. Have you found the saloon yet?'

'No. There are a lot of streets in Framcastle, y'know.'

'Try saying that to the Super. If you find anything, call me at Montoni's at once.'

Jim Martinson held out a cigarette case to the girl. 'It might help if you came with me to Montoni's. I want to talk to that duet, and your introduction would be better than my police card. Don't worry about dress. Montoni's is an informal place. Some call it a joint. Montoni had better watch his step with regard to that little room at the back — '

Jim broke off. 'We could take a taxi if you dislike the idea of riding in a police car,' he said. 'However, the police car is placed at our disposal by the generous ratepayers of Framcastle, whom we endeavour to save from murder, arson and robbery, and the taxi is an infernal machine which eats money.'

'If you're broke, or nearly broke, Montoni's will proceed to break your heart,' said Linda calmly.

'I may be a mere salaried servant,' said Jim stiffly, 'but I can afford to take a girl to Montoni's or any other gilded haunt. Especially when — '

He swallowed. It occurred to him that remarks about a girl's prettiness were something in the nature of a 'line'. Linda Davies would not thank him for outworn cracks. And he'd be a fool to try. She might bracket him as one of those idiots whose first inclination when meeting a girl is to make passes or try out some fatuous routine.

'Especially what?' asked Linda interestedly.

'Oh, I er — guess it would be a great pleasure if you came along,' he said lamely.

'I'll change,' she said. 'Shan't be long.'

He came to the conclusion that Linda was a rare type, for he was surprised when she reappeared in a matter of minutes. She had been as good as her word. She had donned an apple-green dress. He looked at the long evening dress in disgust.

'I hope that doesn't get in the way.'

'Don't you like my dress?' Her voice was cool and, he fancied, slightly distant.

'It's fine, Linda,' he said hastily. 'So

long as we stay at Montoni's. Gosh, you look a bit unapproachable, and I feel rather dusty.' Jim did not inform her that it was his experience that his businesslike outings often developed in queer ways. Once he had ended up in the river. He had got out of that tight spot, for he had not been quite so unconscious as one murderous criminal had imagined.

They left Moor Park Flats and travelled in the swift police car. The uniformed constable who was driving discreetly concentrated on his job. But Jim Martinson had a lot to think about, and not all his thoughts were of the fascinating Linda by his side.

'There's the beginning of a first class mystery in this affair,' he said. 'First we have Jean and she is gadding round with the detestable Lem, and she knows the worst about him apparently. That is a minor mystery. Why did she cotton on to Lem? I can't believe it was because of his charm alone. Major mystery is provided by the riddle of the motive for her murder. And who is the killer? An intriguing point — is he connected with

Lem and the vice ring? I don't know the answer any more than you do, Linda, and that leaves me a heap of work.'

She had her own troubled thoughts. 'I hope there is no threat against June or Elsa. I can't imagine how there can be. What have they done? Oh, when do you think the police will discover poor Jean?'

'They'll not waste time,' he said diplomatically. 'There may be a threat against the other two girls and we can't take chances. Murder is a serious business, and losing my job is another serious business, though perhaps I might make more money selling cars with Ted Delaney. He can buy beer for everybody, and it takes a rich man to do that.'

'Who is Ted Delaney?'

'A pal of mine, I'll introduce you some day. Though — er — perhaps that would be unwise.'

She merely smiled in the subdued light. Jim thought he had never seen a lovelier girl than Linda Davies. Her perfect mouth, those steady eyes — he felt that meeting her was an important moment in his life.

Montoni's club lies in Fenn Street and the entertainment offered is mostly dinner and dance with a cabaret for good measure. The façade of the building is not imposing — a visitor might easily imagine he or she was looking at a prosperous laundry office. But the interior is a concoction of coloured lights, spotless tables and bizarre wall paintings.

Jim took Linda inside, after giving instruction to the police car driver to wait, and seeing that June Carlow and Elsa Mawn were actually giving their show at the moment he secured a table for Linda and himself.

He glanced round. Plenty of uniforms and lounge suits, so his blue serge suit was not too bad. After a hovering waiter attended them, he asked quickly: 'Which is June?'

'Didn't I tell you?' rejoined Linda. 'June is the lighter blonde.'

'Sorry. But I'm only seeking a little corroboration. They look pretty much alike from here. So that is June on Elsa's right.'

Linda sipped at her sherry. 'Yes. And I

shouldn't try to be clever. It is quite easy to be doubtful about who is who from here, but I had the idea that detectives are a sort of super species. If one reads novels, one receives the idea that a detective must be a little strange or a near genius.'

''Fraid I'm just an ordinary chap doing his job. People say I'm lucky.'

June Carlow and Elsa Mawn were average practitioners in the art of syncopated crooning. They were doing a number called, 'I'm Living a Lover's Dream', and Martinson listened politely. At the end, he looked round and grinned at Linda.

'Nice song,' he said. 'What was it all about?'

'Love,' she said, and her voice was severe.

'Oh — that's a universal fault, isn't it?' He had his eyes on the table. 'Well, how do we set about talking to the two girls? Remember we're here on business.'

'And I shouldn't be here at all,' said Linda contritely. 'Poor Jean is dead. Let's go round to June and Elsa's dressing room and talk there.'

They rose and wended their way out of the restaurant towards a passage and Martinson had to wait while Linda went for her wrap. When she reappeared, they proceeded to the regions behind the cabaret stage.

They soon came into contact with the cabaret manager. This harassed individual frowned upon learning that Jim was a detective-inspector.

'Good God, I hope those two kids are not in trouble,' he said fretfully.

Martinson had to console him. 'I merely need information.'

The harassed one escorted them along a crooked passage built of bricks which had been painted instead of panelling or plaster. Soon they came to a door upon which was a number in white, 2.

'Knock and they'll shout.' And unnecessarily he added, 'They've just finished their show.'

Martinson knocked. There was no replying call, so he promptly knocked again.

He waited, one hand on the door

handle. He did not look at Linda. He rapped again, and it was a hard, challenging sound that could be heard all over the bare passage. There was only ominous silence from behind that oak door. Jim tried the handle and found that the door was not locked, yet something was jamming it. He could force it open an inch and that was all. He guessed instantly. A chair was jammed under the door handle inside the room.

He stepped back and then flung his weight against the door. A crack like a dry stick snapping came to his ears and the door moved inwards. Martinson guessed that the chair back had snapped in two, but he wasted little time in such futile reflections.

He was the first inside the room. It was fairly large and warmly decorated — a change from the cold passage — and an assortment of clothes lay in every corner. A draught of cold air eddied through an open window, gently moving the short green curtains. He strode over, looked down onto roofs gleaming dully in the escaping light. The getaway exit, he thought grimly. Linda and the cabaret manager had moved slowly into the room. Jim swung over to examine the two prone bodies even as Linda's horrified gaze fastened immediately upon them.

'June! Elsa!'

She dropped to her knees, stared at their closed eyes.

'Jim! Are they dead?'

Slowly he shook his head. 'No wounds and they are breathing. I think they're doped.' He raised his eyes to the manager. 'Get a doctor. Don't stand gaping.' When the man had darted away, Jim said: 'Someone got away through the open window. They had jammed the door. The girls are drugged, sure enough.'

Linda choked out: 'Why? Someone might have murdered them.'

'Maybe that would have been their ultimate fate,' said Martinson grimly. 'But for the moment someone wanted the two girls alive. Maybe he wanted to make them talk. Who knows?'

He stared through the window. 'They'll have had a car waiting. My knock on the door surprised the man. They'll be two or three streets away by now. If we'd been a little later — '

But Linda was relieved. 'Thank heavens they are only drugged. I think June and Elsa are strong enough to get over the shock pretty soon. If only you had been able to prevent Jean getting into that car . . . '

'Don't rub it in, Linda. You must understand I was acting on the vaguest of suspicions . . . It was merely because I haven't an innocent mind that I went after the girl. Wish I'd got that driver — or a peep at him!'

'You'll get him,' said Linda quietly. 'Got any ideas? I think there is something strange behind these attacks on the three girls.'

Martinson looked up from the silent, deep-sleeping girls as the cabaret manager and another medium sized man in blue overcoat and bowler came quickly into the room.

'The doctor,' said the harassed one.

The medium sized man apparently had no interest in introductions at a time of crisis, for he went immediately on his knees, inspected the prone girls. Within thirty seconds he gave a verdict.

'Rendered insensible by chloroform. They'll come out of it within half an hour.'

June and Elsa were laid on a long sofa and packed up with coats and cushions. 'Have some tea ready for them when they revive,' snapped the doctor. 'I'm afraid I was on my way to a case when this man came to my door.' He indicated the cabaret manager. 'Got to be going.'

'You asked if I had any ideas, Linda,' remarked Jim. 'Well, I can say that the man who was waiting for June and Elsa in this dressing room was well-known to them. Otherwise they would have raised a yell. That seems to be the set-up to me.'

Suddenly a youth came bursting into the room from the passage.

'Message for Inspector Martinson.' Instinctively his eyes went to the towering Martinson. 'Man on 'phone, sir. From Police Headquarters, and he said I could tell you they've found the car. Montoni knows you're here, sir, an' he told me to run along with the message.'

41

'Found the car!' repeated Martinson, and he glanced at Linda. He touched her arm. 'I'd better have a talk with Burrell. I'll let you know — about — Jean.'

And he left her pale and silent.

3

Montoni's Double

'The car was found in an alley down by the riverside streets,' said Detective-Sergeant Burrell. 'The girl is dead — shot. She has been shot through the head at close quarters. Evidently a silencer was used, though the patrol hasn't found the weapon. We're checking up on the car — a fairly well used Parker Superior. It is too much to expect that there'll be obvious clues left lying.'

Martinson listened grimly. 'There's a Big Feller behind this, Stan, and he is not likely to leave paper trails for us. The car will be stolen. You'll run up against a stone wall at a certain point in your investigations. However, better set a man to investigate. I think I'll have a run down to the scene of the crime. Beside Wunter's wharf, you say?'

'Yes. Do you want me down, too?'

'No. Sit tight. Anyway, your missus will expect you home in half-an-hour. I'll attend to everything. Ambulance there?'

'Sure. And a photographer and doctor. They'll just have arrived. I'll let the patrol know you're coming.'

Then Martinson gave his sergeant an account of the attack on June Carlow and Elsa Mawn. It was brief. Then: 'I've met a simply marvellous girl, Stan. She was a friend of the murdered girl.'

'What again?' said Burrell. Then warningly: 'You'd better make sure this Big Feller hasn't anything chalked up for her.'

Jim Martinson came away from the telephone with the warning buzzing in his mind. There was a hard home truth there. He did not think there was the same unknown connection between Linda and Jean Hallison as the one that undoubtedly existed between the dead girl and June and Elsa. But he would not leave that to chance. From now on Linda Davies was in his charge and under his protection, even though it would be more tactful if he never mentioned the fact in concrete terms! The Killer or the Big Feller — what was the best title for him? — had started a murder chain. There was no doubt but for the timely interruption of the dressing room door, June and Elsa would have met Jean Hallison's fate.

Martinson bunched one fist into the other palm. That reasoning brought him again to two questions. What was the motive for the attacks? And who was the Big Feller?

Jim went to see Linda in the dressing room. 'I've got to go down to the riverside streets,' he said. Then quietly: 'Jean has been found — shot.' He gripped her arms. 'I'll not be away long because I feel there'll not be much I can do. The Big Feller is too clever to leave clues in a carefully planned murder. We'll have to get under his cover by some other way. There is always another way.' Jim glanced at the drugged girls, still lying as if in deep sleep. Then, for the first time, he was aware that another man was talking to the cabaret manager.

It was Montoni, the owner and originator of the club. Martinson grinned over to him. Tony Montoni — heaven only knew if that was his correct name — was almost as big as himself. Almost, but not quite. Jim was willing to wager that he could give Montoni a good many pounds and at least three inches. Then, again, Montoni supped and wined too well and no doubt he indulged in other excesses as well. Even so he was a big man.

'Inspector Martinson — you must keep this little incident quiet. It is hardly the best publicity for my club,' and Tony Montoni smiled. His eyes were jet black and held many glints. When he smiled he showed fine white teeth. His dark hair grew thick and strayed into long side-boards. His cheeks were large and he had large red lips.

An interesting character, Martinson thought. He knew Montoni claimed the protection of British citizenship, but the truth was he was a man without a country. Turkey, Spain or Italy would not recognise him, or grant him repatriation. So he was a British subject and no doubt thankful. The police knew Montoni was ready to step over the boundary line of law and order if the stakes were enticing and the proposition safe.

'As it happens, Montoni, it will be kept quiet. There is nothing to be gained by broadcasting it,' retorted Martinson.

Jim turned to Linda. 'Keep an eye on the girls while I'm away — but I don't have to tell you that. Especially I want you to repeat to me anything they say when they first come round. I'll send a uniformed policeman to be your body-guard — just in case.'

Martinson left Montoni's club and in the police car sped down to the river. They rushed by tall dark buildings, some of which were derelict while others still housed large office suites and warehouses. They came to the grimy river where the cold wind blew; but it was hardly strong enough to dispel the odours of the alleys.

They found Wunter's wharf and in a dark street nearby two cars were station-ary. One was a police car and the other, Martinson soon perceived as he approached, was the blue saloon. There was a pool of light from headlights, and in another adjoin-ing alley Martinson saw the ambulance.

Half-a-dozen loafers stood in the shadows, looking on furtively at a scene that aroused no feeling in their hearts except curiosity.

Martinson got through the investigation rapidly. He was not disposed to dawdle, and additionally there was no need. He wanted to get some of the four cars away. The ambulance was first off, taking the body of Jean Hallison. A detective constable took some photographs, and when his flash lit up the scene, some of the loafers melted away magically.

Martinson knew that checking the car and looking for weapons was a mere matter of routine. He was looking for something significant no matter how tiny and the first thing was to examine the car thoroughly.

Surely the girl had put up a struggle when she realised the journey was a fake? Just whether she'd been killed at this very spot or whether the murderer had shot her earlier, was difficult to say. It seemed, in this case, the murderer was a paid underling of the Big Feller. If Jean

Hallison had struggled before the callous swine had carried out his orders, there was the possibility of some scrap of evidence. It might be microscopic and yet valuable.

With a pocket lamp, which he borrowed from the patrol car, he looked into every nook and cranny of the blue saloon. It was a long way from being a new car, and many surprising items, possibly belonging to previous owners, came to light. Martinson was quite sure investigations would prove the car to be stolen and possibly just recently, and in that case the odd things found did not necessarily link up with the Big Feller or his underlings.

He found two playing cards, a generous assortment of bread and cake crumbs, a green matchstick, several cigarette ends, a specimen flag from an orphanage flag day. These items were in and around the upholstery. In the door pockets he found another playing card with the same green dragon emblazoned upon the back, a cigarette packet of popular make and a dog-racing fixture card.

The discoveries might belong to anybody.

Jim Martinson memorised the items, placed them in separate envelopes, which were again supplied by the patrol car — and sealed them.

'Take the car to Police Headquarters garage,' he told the uniformed men in the patrol car. 'Wear gloves when handling her. There may be fingerprints. I'm putting the experts on at Headquarters, and we'll pull this car to pieces if need be.'

There was nothing more to be done in this dark street. The ambulance was away, and now the blue saloon was to be towed to Headquarters for further examination. Martinson swung into his police car, told the driver to return to Montoni's club. Then they were gone. The shadowy loafers retreated to their haunts and the street was deserted, only to be visited periodically by two policemen on their lonely beat.

Martinson got to Montoni's, and his big figure strode swiftly down passages to the dressing room. He rapped and went in. Linda Davies was talking cheerfully to the two girls. Both girls were balancing teacups in their hands, and as they sipped, the warm liquid chased away the sickly pallor in their faces.

Martinson smiled encouragingly. Linda rose to meet him, and he drew her to one side. 'Nothing can be done for Jean Hallison,' he said quietly. 'Don't worry. Let's see if we can cheer up these two girls. What did they say when they first came round?'

After a moment of silence she said slowly: 'Nothing that made sense. Mostly sighs and exclamations like 'Oh, dear'. I listened very carefully, but that was all Elsa and June said.'

Martinson tapped her arm, and she turned with him and approached the pale singers. Jim sat down and said: 'My name's Jim Martinson. I'm a detective-inspector from Framcastle C.I.D. There's one big question I would like answered — Who was the man who attacked you? What did he look like?'

They did not speak. He did not fail to notice the look of fright in their faces as they glanced at each other.

'Come on,' urged Jim. 'The sooner I

get the information, the sooner the police will lay their hands on the man.'

June Carlow's oval face stared up, her shrewd eyes were full of uncertainty.

'You won't have to go far,' she said suddenly.

Elsa protested. 'June! We were seeing things. It couldn't have been . . . '

'But it was,' snapped June. Her bright eyes turned to Jim. 'Montoni was in the room. He attacked us. We never expected it. But it's mad — mad! He's the best boss we've ever had. I don't know why I'm telling you this. We've been wondering whether we should keep it to ourselves.'

4

Explanations

'So Montoni was waiting for you — and he attacked you. Very surprising!' Martinson muttered. But his brain was racing a long way ahead of 'surprises'.

'Montoni was waiting for us,' repeated June Carlow. 'We came tearing in as we usually do, and he grinned at us and rose. I was just going to say, 'Okay, Montoni, what's on your mind?' when he put his big arms round Elsa and me. The next thing I realised was a peculiar sweet smell. Montoni was between us and had an arm round each of us. At first I thought he was larking, you know. Then his grip became terribly strong. I couldn't break away. He was holding a pad in each hand — I had about a second to notice that much — and then the dopey smelling pad was over my mouth. I just went under as if it was knockout drops, I guess.'

'You could not have made a mistake?'

'Listen, Inspector, it was Montoni. We know Montoni when we see him.'

'Yes, he is rather outstanding, but all the same it wasn't Montoni who tried to dope you.'

He ignored their gasps. He went to the door, opened it, spoke to the uniformed constable who had been stationed there during the time Martinson had been down at Wunter's wharf.

'See if you can get Montoni, constable. You see,' said Martinson, coming back to the girls, 'I happened to notice Montoni in the restaurant while you were doing your show. He was still there when Linda and I left the table to come and see you in your dressing room.'

'But this is incredible,' said Linda, and her eyes questioned him. She gave a short laugh. 'You'll tell us next that Montoni has a double. I think I've read about such things in novels.'

Jim Martinson shook his head. He said: 'I don't know if Montoni has a double. I should think it very unlikely. But it seems some individual put up a good imitation act tonight.' Jim was wandering round the dressing room peering at pots of makeup, photographs and, unashamedly, articles of feminine attire. His hands were in his pockets. Linda thought his back seemed broader than ever. 'I think,' began Jim, and then came a knock. In two strides he stepped across the dressing room, opened the door. Montoni and the constable entered.

Tony Montoni grinned. 'Now you want my advice, eh? Ah-ha, how is June and Elsa? You do not look well. You are pale. I think you should go home and rest.'

They stared in silence. Their lack of response caused him to raise his eyebrows. He was about to break into more rapid speech when Jim interposed.

'Tony, the girls say you attacked them in this room with a chloroform pad. What do you say?'

Montoni went through a range of emotions, which were almost ludicrous. His red lips pouted, his cheeks expanded and his eyes were alternately amazed and beseeching. Jim grinned at the performance and waited.

'What you say? I attack girls — that is

monstrous — monstrous! They do not know what they say — it is impossible — because I was not here!' — this triumphantly — 'Ah-ha, I remember, I was in the restaurant just after the girls' show. A lot of my good friends will tell you they saw me. So I could not do this — this terrible thing to June and Elsa.'

'I'm afraid you couldn't,' said Martinson. 'For one thing, I can vouch for your story, and no doubt there are dozens of other people who could do the same. It's a frame-up.'

'You mean it wasn't Montoni?' shrilled June Carlow.

'Couldn't have been. Tony has a cast iron alibi. Anyway, it is an obvious set-up. Actually it doesn't stand up to a little applied logic. If Montoni wanted to dope you two girls, he'd hardly set about the business so crudely giving you every opportunity to identify him.'

Montoni puffed out his cheeks. 'I tell you — it is not my nature — Ah, no, Tony Montoni would never stoop to attack so beautiful ladies. No, no, no.'

Jim Martinson thought: 'There are quite

a few discreditable episodes in your life, though.'

'Well, you got a double, Montoni.' declared June Carlow.

The other shook his head vigorously. 'I know nothing about this double. He must be a scoundrel. Inspector, I hope you put your hands on him quickly.'

Jim brought out his cigarettes, handed them round

'Who actually attacked June and Elsa, Jim?' asked Linda.

Martinson said promptly: 'A man of Montoni's build, painted, wigged and disguised to look like Montoni. Doubles — true doubles — exist mostly among ordinary-looking people. Two Tony Montonis in this city would be too much of a coincidence. The whole thing boils down to a stunt to bewilder me, and of course, it was necessary that June and Elsa should not be alarmed when they entered their dressing room.'

'Well, I'm going home,' said June Carlow suddenly. 'Elsa, a good eight hours sleep would be like a bit of heaven. Coming?'

The other girl nodded. They put away the teacups, looked round the dressing room. Montoni suddenly became the energetic nightclub owner again. 'I must go,' he said. 'So much to do.' He made for the door. Martinson watched him go. Then he said to the singers:

'I'll take you home in a police car. I'd like to ask you a few questions.'

'About what?'

'Have you any idea why you should be attacked? You know, of course, that Jean Hallison is dead?'

'Yes,' said June in a subdued tone. 'Linda told us after we had recovered. Poor Jean.'

'Why should she be murdered? Can you imagine a reason, however slight?'

He looked at them, saw beneath their sophistication they were frightened kids.

June said in a low voice: 'I can't imagine why Jean was murdered. Oh, I know she was playing the fool at times, but — murder! There's a madman about. I know damn well it was a near thing for us.'

Martinson said cheerfully: 'Well, from

now on you'll have two big policemen hanging round your door. There'll be no more near things.'

He felt far from satisfied with the information he'd unearthed. He was a long way from discovering a motive for the killing of Jean Hallison. Of course, motive and identity were often bound together.

Jim shrugged. 'If everyone is ready,' he said, 'we'll get down to the car.'

'I hope it is a big car,' said Elsa impishly.

'Big enough for one bloke and three girls,' returned Martinson, and he grinned hugely at Linda.

Presently they made their way down the passage. They were nearly beside the entrance when June Carlow said inconsequentially: 'That is Montoni's private office.' She indicated the richly panelled door with the thick frosted glass.

Martinson halted. 'I'll let him know we're going.'

He knocked and a muffled voice bade him enter.

He opened the door, walked in easily.

Within seconds he got a photographic impression of the office and its occupants. The place was richly furnished, carpets were thick and the fireplace big and luxurious. Even with the unobtrusive desk, the room looked more like a lounge than an office.

There were three people sitting at a table. One was Montoni and he glanced up with a grin while his fingers flicked at a pack of cards. Opposite Montoni was a woman. Jim Martinson had never seen her before but he knew instantly that he would not easily forget her.

She was not a girl, yet she had a dark mature beauty, which should have no fear of competition. She was tall. She was as tall as Linda, Martinson thought, but her height gave the impression of power whereas Linda's height accentuated her girlishness. Martinson noted her clothes. They were expensive, he guessed. Her emerald dress came down to faultless shoes, her rich sealskin covered three-quarters of her dress.

Jim could absorb details with the speed of a camera. He glanced at the other man, sitting beside the woman.

He looked conventional. Dark, urbane. his evening clothes fitting him exactly. He had crinkled, carefully tended hair and a curt moustache. He calmly stared towards Martinson.

Within seconds of Martinson's appearance, Montoni began to talk rapidly.

'Aha, Inspector. Again you come to see me. Allow me to introduce my friends — Mrs. Pelham — Detective-Inspector Martinson. Inspector — Mr. Edmund Falconer.'

Jim murmured: 'So delighted! Sorry to butt in, Tony. Merely wanted to say I'm away, taking the girls home.'

Montoni grinned, showing white teeth. 'You are a lucky man, Inspector.' Tony flashed the cards through his fingers. 'Have you any new clues?'

'I'm afraid not,' drawled Jim. He was looking at the cards. He could distinctly see the green dragon emblazoned on their backs.

He remembered he'd found three similar cards in the murder car.

5

Body in the River

To Detective-Inspector Martinson the swift journey home was uneventful, with three girls sitting in the roomy back seat and himself beside the police driver. Linda was taken to her flat and June and Elsa deposited at their home in Highbourne. Two extra policemen came silently to Oval Drive and spent the night looking for suspicious passers by.

Jim Martinson felt uncertain about the possibility of danger to Linda Davies, but he was taking no chances. The Big Feller had hinted that there were others apart from Jean Hallison. Did that mean Linda might be attacked? He placed another constable at Moor Park Flats.

He wondered to whom the green dragon cards belonged. It was likely they belonged to Montoni's nightclub, but who had been so careless as to leave three cards in the pockets of the murder car?

Jim Martinson went home to rest and found his bed more pleasure than it had been for some time. He was tired, yet he lay thinking of Linda. Now if he could only marry a girl like that, he could leave his digs forever. It sounded a fine idea.

Next morning at the Police Headquarters he found Lem Dallas had been hauled in on some obscure charge. Jim had the man brought up from the cells.

'Hello, Lem. Pretty bad, isn't it, Lem, that the little girl you were with last night was murdered?'

He knew Lem had not seen the morning paper. He wondered if Lem would reveal that he knew Jean Hallison was dead, for Lem had not been told why he had been hauled in.

The little dancehall rat stood and glowered.

'Aren't you talking, Lem?'

'I don't know anything about Jean being murdered!' burst out Lem. 'An' you can't keep me here — you've got to make a charge and you've got nothing on me.'

'Why conclude I was talking about Jean

Hallison? I merely said 'the little girl you were with'. So you knew Jean Hallison would be murdered?'

'I didn't know anything of the sort!' snarled Lem.

'Who was the driver of that car which took the girl away last night?' Jim rapped across his desk.

'I don't know!'

'You tell me and I'll promise to go easy with you when we get the real evidence lined up against you,' said Jim softly.

'So you got nothing against me now,' said Lem triumphantly. 'Let me outa here, Mister Martinson, or I'll summon the police for wrongful arrest.'

Jim looked at the other in surprise. 'Why, Mr. Dallas, we merely took you in for your own protection. Your friend, Jean Hallison, has been murdered, and who knows — you might be in danger.'

Lem Dallas buttoned his tight-fitting jacket and smoothed his hair.

'Gimme a pass-out from this place. I don't want protection. If I went to a lawyer, he could smash that yarn to pieces.'

'Keep away from lawyers, Lem,' said Jim.

A police constable escorted Lem to the ornate entrance of the new, huge Police Headquarters. Even as Lem stepped to the pavement outside, Jim Martinson was instructing a detective to spend the day watching Lem.

'If he leads you to anything interesting, ring me up.'

There was routine work waiting for Martinson and with the help of Detective-Sergeant Burrell, he waded through the office work.

A report came in concerning the murder car. The car had been stolen, and belonged to a city businessman. There were many fingerprints but none were identifiable with known criminals. Most of the fingerprints probably belonged to the rightful owner.

The car owner had stated that the objects found in the car, such as the orphanage flag and the dog racing programme, were left by him. But the owner knew nothing about the three green dragon cards. He had never seen them before, according to his statement.

'A little thing,' murmured Martinson,

scanning the report. 'Now I wonder if Montoni has a monopoly of this make of card?'

Martinson sent a man over to make the inquiry. Half-an-hour later the detective returned.

'Montoni says the cards can be bought at one or two city shops. I checked that. Sanson's have some for sale. But Montoni has a few packs, which he blandly states are used for games of rummy and patience with which he passes an odd hour.'

'Just as likely he uses the cards at his gaming parties in that cute back room of his,' commented Martinson.

The card clue wasn't very conclusive and Martinson put it to one side.

Towards the end of an arduous day of office work, Jim Martinson received a call from the detective who had spent an unenviable day trailing Lem Dallas.

'Lem was inside a billiard hall all the morning. I managed to eat in an adjoining café. He spent up to three o'clock in a pub, and then went along to an afternoon dance at the Palais de Danse. I came out with him. He was talking to a girl. He spent some time giving her slick talk and I bet he was making a date. After that he walked down to the riverside streets. He is now inside Sally Skipp's café. I am watching from this telephone booth.'

'A day in the life of friend Lem,' commented Martinson. 'Well George, hang on until I come down. I'd like to watch Lem a little myself. Somehow I think he'll lead us to something. Though it is just a vague hunch, I believe Lem is the link between us and the killer. I think Lem knows the killer, and I think he is the big man who runs the vice racket up and down the river.'

'I'll hang on until you are down, sir,' said the detective.

Jim Martinson travelled the mile to the riverside street in a police car, and then he instructed the driver to return to Headquarters. Jim walked the length of the grimy ramshackle thoroughfare and encountered the patient detective standing in a doorway a good bit removed from Sally Skipp's café.

'Lem is still inside the café,' said the detective.

'Good. Do you think he knows we're watching him?'

'I've been pretty careful. I don't think he has seen me.'

'Righto, George. You buzz off to your family circle. You have had an unexciting day, and I'll probably have an unexciting night, but one never knows. Sooner or later Lem might try to contact his boss.'

The detective grinned and sauntered away.

It was a dreary, cold evening, which would soon turn dark. Jim Martinson buttoned the collar of his thick ulster and pulled his hat down over his eyes. The worst of being known to one's prey was that it made impossible a direct approach

Jim's vigil was self-imposed. He could have gone home or sat in a warm theatre. But Martinson had a one-track mind, and while the Big Feller threatened two or three girls with death, he would spend all his time on the case.

It was a safe bet that sooner or later Lem Dallas would link up with his boss. Jim Martinson was inclining more to the view that the Big Feller was the unknown vice organiser and the murderer of Jean

68

Hallison. Why Jean had been murdered, he still did not know.

Tonight there would be a guard on Moor Park Flats, and June and Elsa would have police protection while they travelled to Montoni's nightclub. The Big Feller might find it more difficult to carry out his threats.

Jim Martinson stepped back into the doorway and half-turned his head. Two men had stepped out of Sally Skipp's rough café and were walking slowly along the road.

Martinson recognised Lem Dallas instantly. His recognition of the other man surprised him.

Lem was accompanied by Mr. Edmund Falconer.

Martinson busied himself with a cigarette while the other two walked slowly past, on the other side of the road.

Edmund Falconer was warmly clad in an expensive overcoat and hat. He was talking carefully to Lem Dallas. Martinson waited until they reached the end of the street, and then he moved slowly after them.

He was agreeably surprised at the turn of events. If only he knew what conversation was passing between them! Also he would like to learn how Edmund Falconer knew Lem. Perhaps Montoni had remarked upon the attack delivered in his premises upon his two cabaret girls, but did Montoni know about Lem? The morning papers gave an account of the murder of Jean Hallison, but mentioned nothing of Lem Dallas.

Jim Martinson walked slowly down the street and when Lem and Edmund Falconer turned the corner, he hurried a little. He caught sight of them again as they turned along the quayside.

He wondered if Lem was taking Edmund Falconer to some place or vice versa.

The two men went to a flight of stone stairs, which led from the quay down into the muddy water of the great industrial river. As their heads disappeared, Martinson walked quickly towards the edge of the quay. He skirted a stationary railway wagon and looked down at the river, nearly one hundred yards higher up the river from the stairs.

He saw Lem and Edmund Falconer step into a small motorboat. It was a grimy vessel without an inch of decent paint. Lem was evidently busy with the engine, while Falconer stood and watched. Occasionally he turned his head to survey the surrounding river, and Martinson moved away.

Lem and the other man were taking a trip on the river but it would hardly be a pleasure trip. Soon dusk would fall in its murky fashion over the river district. Where was Lem going?

Jim wondered if the motorboat belonged to Lem or Edmund Falconer. If it belonged to Falconer, then the man had evidently intended to meet Lem. Who was Falconer, anyway?

Martinson hurried along the quay, moving away from the spot where Lem and Falconer stood in the motorboat. Martinson was well aware that a river police station lay near to the suspension bridge.

He did not bother to enter the station building, but went down some steps to where a river-police launch bobbed in the choppy river.

A uniformed constable stood in the diminutive deck of the craft. Martinson stepped aboard and hailed the man.

'Hello, Wilson.'

The river policeman grinned.

'Hello, Inspector. Nice night for a walk.'

'Be a confoundedly murky night in another few hours. What about taking me down the river for a few minutes in this boat? There are two queer blokes — at least one is — and I'd like to learn something about them.'

The river policeman promptly cranked the marine engine. The petrol engine started immediately. Martinson turned his collar closer and stood in the cockpit of the craft. Within a few seconds the boat moved away from the jetty.

Jim Martinson had no control over the river police, but he knew the constable as well as he knew a few hundred others who patrolled the streets of Framcastle. Martinson told the constable about the grimy motorboat containing the two men.

Within a few minutes Martinson spotted the craft containing Lem and his friend. He gave orders to the river policeman to proceed at dead slow speed.

'The great idea is to see where those two are going, Wilson. That's all I've got in mind at the moment. One of the men left the Headquarters cell this morning. I suspect he is mixed up with a particularly nasty murder.'

'The girl who was shot in the car?' queried Wilson.

Martinson nodded.

The river policeman deftly kept the launch idling against the fast moving river. Martinson watched Lem's grey-black boat bob over the river, moving swiftly downstream. After a discreet distance was separating the two craft, the river policeman allowed the launch to move slowly after the other.

Apparently Lem had not noticed the distant police launch, or, if he had, it did not worry him. The grimy motorboat slipped past barges and decayed wharfs, and then came up against a large motorboat tied at the side of the river, close to an old barge.

'Don't go up to them, Wilson,' said Jim.

The engine was cut, and the constable turned the boat towards the riverbank. Martinson saw the two men climb from the grimy boat and board the larger craft. They evidently tied their vessel to the other boat, and then disappeared into the interior of the bigger craft.

'Land me at the river bank,' said Martinson. 'Strictly speaking this is not your show. I'll walk down the river bank, see what is going on from there.'

'We could board — if we had a warrant,' said Wilson.

'We've got nothing but my suspicious mind,' said Martinson.

Jim landed on the derelict riverbank, and the police launch turned and slipped upstream. Jim walked along in the gathering murky evening. The path was a mere track, passing ruins of old warehouses and factories. It was a dreary scene, a blighted, forgotten area of decaying rubble and jetties.

He sauntered along until he was standing on the riverbank looking at the tied up barge and the launch that lay alongside. There seemed to be little activity on board the big launch, and those inside displayed no lights.

Jim Martinson spent some ten minutes watching the big motorboat, wondering to whom it belonged and why Lem Dallas and Edmund Falconer had visited the craft. Did the boat belong to Falconer? Why bother to visit the boat? If they had something to talk about, surely they could talk in Sally Skipp's café?

After the ten minutes elapsed, Martinson got tired of waiting. He came round the broken wall, which had served as a cover point, and saw that he could climb on to the old barge.

It was the work of a minute to jump the six-feet gap from the crumbling quay to the barge. Martinson stood beside the hatch, which led down into a filthy, mysterious hole inside the barge. This grimy apartment had once been the bargee's retreat from the cold river winds.

Even as Jim paused, staring at the tied-up motorboat in the gathering gloom, he heard a noise of footsteps coming from the adjoining boat. In a second he guessed some one was about to emerge on to the small deck of the motorboat. Martinson did not want to be seen. He promptly lowered himself through the open hatch, found some iron rungs and climbed down carefully. The operation was a matter of seconds, and he stood hidden with only his eyes and head showing above the barge deck.

He had hidden himself just in time, for two men appeared on the deck of the motorboat. They were carrying a man between them! The two men worked very quickly — so quickly that Martinson was unable to discover the identity of the man. He had never seen the two men before, either. He did perceive that the man they carried did not struggle. The next instant the two men, after a quick glance up and down the deserted river, pushed the body over the side of the motorboat into the river.

Jim Martinson uttered a rough exclamation. He watched the two men quickly dive into the boat cabin. Martinson made up his mind on the spur of the moment.

He hauled himself from the narrow barge hatch, ran aft down the barge. His keen eyes caught a momentary glimpse of a dark, bobbing body on the surface of the river. Martinson plunged over the side. He wasted no time in a deep dive, but kicked out strongly with a powerful crawl stroke. The river was taking the man downstream swiftly.

Martinson was a strong swimmer, and a few minutes later had need to be. He grabbed the collar of the floating man and began to haul him to the bank. Against the current it was an accomplishment for any swimmer. The biting cold stabbed at Jim Martinson. His clothes felt like a lead belt. Then, as the choppy river swirled them, he saw the face of the man he was rescuing.

It was Lem Dallas. He seemed unconscious.

Martinson reached the riverbank with numb limbs and a grim feeling. He crawled through slime towards harder ground, lugging Lem Dallas with him. Jim began to shiver as cold river air blew against his sodden clothes.

Then he stopped to examine Lem Dallas for the first time.

He cursed. He looked back at the motorboat beside the barge. The boat was nearly a hundred yards away.

Martinson stared down at Lem again. The man was undoubtedly dead. Jim had rescued a dead man. For the dead man's clothes had been ripped from his chest and there was a ghastly wound.

Martinson knew it had been inflicted with a knife. In the river, the wound had been hidden by the water.

Jim Martinson left Lem Dallas on the hard riverbank, and made his way towards the barge. For one thing, he would like the ulster, which he had ripped off as he dived into the river. It would serve to keep away the icy wind. And another thing: he longed grimly to learn who was inside the big motorboat.

Martinson wished he could contact the river police in a few seconds, but this desolate stretch of river was bare of human beings or houses. He wished he had one of the latest walkie-talkie radio sets. They would stand even immersion in the river. He wished he had not sent Wilson away.

He was near to the barge when the two men who had thrown Lem Dallas in the river appeared from round the crumbling wall on the derelict quay. They were not ten yards distant. Martinson paused, cursing.

'That's 'im — left his coat — been in the river — '

Jim Martinson felt that a scrap would keep the blood tingling in his veins. As it was he was shivering.

His fist rammed one ruffian's nose and Martinson followed with another blow, which slogged sickeningly into the man's face. They were blows that should have felled any ordinary man. But the riverside thug was inured to knocks. He grunted and staggered, but one fist rammed into Martinson's middle.

The other man jumped to deal Jim a foul blow, but Martinson jerked instinctively, ramming his fist out like a piston.

But two men are difficult to fight, especially when they are hard-bitten thugs. Martinson slogged away, dodging by the skin of his teeth many vicious kicks and attempts to drag him to the ground.

Jim wished someone would come along the riverbank, but he was well aware that this desolate site was avoided. Now, with dusk falling, the entire riverbank was no man's land.

In truth his blood was tingling, but he realised the two men were hard cases. Martinson felt sure he could lay them out one at a time and in succession, but they were not obliging.

For Martinson, the end came when a man ran from the motorboat, over the deck of the barge, and approached the three fighting men.

The man was Edmund Falconer, and he held a gun in his hand Jim saw him running. He tried to leap away from the two attacking thugs. He realised he was in a tight corner.

Falconer did not shoot. He closed with Martinson and for a moment added to the weight of the attack against the big man. Then Falconer saw the opportunity he wanted. He got under Jim's guard. His hand swung and he brought the butt end of the gun down with a ghastly crack against Martinson's head.

Jim sagged slowly and even as he fell the three men began to drag him down to the water's edge.

'In the river?' grated one thug.

Falconer said: 'No. We'll put him in the barge. We'll have to listen to what the boss says.'

6

Death by Knife

Edmund Falconer did not soil his hands by helping the two thugs with the dirty work. He simply accompanied the two men while they hauled Jim Martinson to the barge and dropped him inside the dirty compartment.

Then with quick actions the three men climbed down into the motorboat. They walked into the cabin, closing the sliding door after them. Inside the cabin they halted and faced the figure sitting at a table at the distant end. Falconer's actions gave the impression of an amount of respect equal to that of the two thugs, though his was not the awe arising out of ignorance.

'So you got Martinson,' commented the figure in a husky voice.

The scene might have been fantastic, but the three men facing the figure wore serious expressions. Sitting at the table was a person of medium height clad in a voluminous green cloak, which covered the body head to foot. That there was a reason for this masquerade was plain to see. The cloak disguised the form, figure, and even the character of the person. The formless cloak, with its hood bearing slits for eyes and mouth, was a first-class disguise for anyone wishing to conceal their identity.

'The dick is inside the barge, Boss,' jerked one of the thugs.

'I know. I watched you. Have you thrown Lem's body back into the river?'

'No.' The thug gave reluctant response. Even Falconer bit his lip. He knew instantly they would hear sarcastic comments.

'Then do it at once. And when you are throwing him back, reflect upon the fate of traitors and fools.'

As the thug turned rapidly and left the cabin, Falconer said: 'What do you propose we should do with Martinson? We left him in the barge pending your decision.'

The Boss, or as Jim Martinson would call him, the Big Feller, sat motionless for a few seconds before replying. Then:

'Martinson is becoming a nuisance. This is an opportunity to get rid of him. Fire the inside of that barge. I believe it is full of inflammable rubbish, and a charred body found later is not identifiable.'

Falconer nodded.

'That method is as good as any.' He half turned. The Big Feller spoke again in that abrupt, husky voice.

'I want to talk to you, Edmund. Salter, you fire the inside of the barge, and when your big colleague returns, take the launch down to the River House.'

The other thug nodded and hurried away.

When the sliding door had closed again, the Big Feller said: 'You know, Edmund, Lem and that girl were becoming grave menaces to me. They had guessed at my identity, you see.'

Falconer nodded again, conscious that he was one — in fact the only one now — of those who knew the Boss's identity.

It seemed the Big Feller had read his thoughts.

'Unlike you, Edmund, they were not people I could trust. Well, when the other two return, we'll get back to River House. I have many things to attend to, including a visit by Ali Mohammad. It seems he is in need of some girls.'

★　★　★

Jim Martinson stirred painfully. His eyes were closed tightly and nightmarish images floated in deep chasms of black space. His head ached, and every part of him seemed stiff with icy cold. He was crawling on his hands and feet wondering why his lungs seemed almost choking with the effort of breathing. He found a wall and clawed at the surface. He found a grip and hauled himself to his feet standing dizzily in a sickening black world of pain and choking fumes.

He wrenched his eyes open. At first it seemed the muscles had lost control; then with open eyes his brain began to grasp facts as he reeled round in gloom.

The overwhelming fact was the air was thick with suffocating fumes. Jim beat at the wall, discovered he was hammering at ships' planking and it came to him in a flash that he was inside the old barge. Fumes stung his eyes and he closed them again. He blundered round, seeking the iron ladder leading out of the barge compartment.

He remembered his fight with the two thugs, and Falconer joining in. He remembered the instantaneous pain and darkness that had descended upon his head. He wondered how long he had been unconscious. He thanked his lucky star his skull was thick.

He found the ladder and began to climb. Though he could not see in the gloom, he visualised the air being full of smoke. He could see no fire, but the smoke burned his throat and lungs.

At the top of the iron ladder Martinson found the hatch-cover immovable. Someone had battened him down. He pushed first with one hand. Then, in desperation, he braced himself and hammered with both fists. He continued the work, fancying the wood might yield, but after an intense period of struggle, during which he spiked his hands on rusty nails and nearly fell from the ladder, he realised the hatch was solidly fixed.

He climbed down the ladder. The smoke was unbearable. He must discover from where it was issuing and stop it. He stumbled over the compartment, coughing, his eyes streaming. He immediately blundered into a heap of rubbish, and as his feet disturbed the stuff, a red glow suddenly flared in the centre of the heap.

Jim realised that he had been left to burn inside the barge, but, by a million-to-one chance the rubbish had died down into a smouldering pile. Perhaps the man who had carried out the job had been careless and had not noticed that some of the rubbish was damp.

He scattered the heap with his feet, carefully stamping upon any stuff that seemed ready to burst into flame. Soot, filth and smoke rose in the air. Jim felt he must seek fresh air, and he nearly left his task of stamping out the smouldering remains. How he could get to fresh air, he did not know. It was simply a blind urge to run from the suffocating smoke. He fought the mad impulse, stamping round in the gloom, beating the fire out of the smouldering rubbish.

He was suddenly excited a moment later. His foot had encountered a short iron bar at the bottom of the rubbish pile. He plunged his hand among the warm ashes, raised the bar to his height.

It was about four feet long and seemed to be a piece of angle iron. Perhaps it had once been used somewhere in the barge and then dumped in this compartment to be forgotten.

Jim Martinson used it as a battering ram. He climbed the iron ladder again, and rammed the angle iron at the wooden hatch. The first blow achieved more than he could have hoped for with bare hands. The second blow brought the welcome sound of wood cracking to Jim's ears. He hammered away, gulping air at each swing of the heavy iron bar.

At last one blow carried the bar right through the hatch cover, and, following with another triumphant thud, Jim knocked aside a whole plank in the cover. After that, breathing fresh river air, it was simply a matter of steady work to clear a hole large enough for him to haul himself to the barge deck. He sat for a few seconds gasping at cold, clean air.

'Nearly, my friend, but not quite!' he murmured.

The motorboat had vanished. A grey, misty murk had settled over the riverside, and there was no movement to be seen anywhere. Jim could not find his ulster, and concluded it had been flung into the barge to burn with him.

He did not intend to enter the compartment again. He jumped the gap to the shore and forced his stiff limbs into a run. He arrived at a police telephone box on the fringe of the inhabited streets near to the desolate shore.

He 'phoned Police Headquarters. In less than five minutes a police car tore up and stopped at the police box. Martinson got in, shivering. 'Take me to my digs in Meriton Street, Dick,' he said. 'I admit it — I've had enough for tonight.'

But when he arrived at his digs he used

his telephone for a long time. He put into motion the entire river police organization in an effort to find the mystery motorboat.

Martinson bathed and changed into a tweed suit. He was drinking tea when Ted Delaney called.

Ted was sporting a new suit. It was a rather striking creation of chocolate and chalk stripes, and Ted's chubby face bore a look of expectancy when he entered Martinson's rooms. He took off his overcoat, and grinned at Jim Martinson.

'Beautiful!' murmured Jim. 'You look like the leading man in a musical comedy.'

'Is that so?' demanded Ted, and he punched the other in the ribs.

Jim rubbed his side tenderly.

'You shouldn't do that. I've been mauled enough today.'

He had to tell his friend the events that followed the trailing of Lem Dallas. In fact, in rapid sentences he soon gave Ted the whole story commencing with his meeting Jean Hallison at the Palais de Danse.

'Perhaps you'll let me see Linda before you become irretrievably involved in Cupid's gambles,' said Ted.

Jim Martinson eyed the other's suit. 'I think it will be safe enough with you in those duds.'

Ted nearly punched him again. Instead he stroked Jim on the back with an exaggerated air of solicitude.

The telephone rang. Jim put his cup of tea to one side.

'Martinson speaking.'

'This is Stan Burrell. Jim, one of the cabaret girls has disappeared. The one called Elsa Mawn. They were escorted to Montoni's club in Fenn Street, and then Elsa slipped out before she changed. Her partner says the girl must have slipped out for cigarettes. Anyway, she vanished. Now don't come over, if you are not feeling like it, Jim. I've heard all about the affair down the river.'

'I'm feeling fine,' Jim paused. 'Is Miss Davies under strict guard, Stan?'

'I've got a man stationed inside the main passage of those flats, and another outside.'

91

'Good. Well, I'll pop over to Montoni's club.

'Righto. I'm going over myself. See you there.'

Jim turned to Ted.

'Have you got that Riley outside?'

'At your service,' said Ted Delaney.

'You could take me over to Montoni's nightclub and I'll forgive you dazzling my eyes with that suit,' said Martinson.

The short journey through crowded city streets did not give Ted much opportunity to show his driving skill so far as speed was concerned, though he gave a slick demonstration of traffic driving. Within a few minutes they pulled into the car park behind Montoni's club. Martinson and Ted went in to see Tony Montoni.

Detective-Sergeant Burrell had got there before Jim simply because the Police Headquarters were not far from Fenn Street. Jim found him in Montoni's luxurious office with the proprietor of the nightclub.

'Hello, Stan. Got any facts?'

'The girl slipped out to buy something,'

said Burrell. 'She has simply vanished, according to Montoni and June Carlow.'

Montoni nodded his big head.

'Yes — the show is ruined! One girl — that is no good. Poor Elsa, this scoundrel man has got her!'

Jim took Ted and Stan Burrell along to see June Carlow in her dressing room, and he found a scared girl who had dressed in her street clothes again. Jim Martinson asked:

'Why should Elsa go outside? Couldn't she send a messenger?'

'Elsa was like that,' said June, 'she knew all day the police had set a guard to watch us, and then I suppose she forgot all about it. Must have been an impulse. She did not say anything to me. I knew she had left the dressing room, but that is nothing. She has not returned.'

'Let's get outside,' muttered Martinson. 'Stan, where is the constable who travelled over with the two girls from their home to this place?'

'He should be on duty, outside the place.'

They found the constable who had

travelled over with Elsa and June. He was a worried man, for already he knew one of his charges had disappeared.

'I swear she never passed this way, sir,' he said. 'I'd have stopped her. She never passed me, sir.'

'She could have left by some side door,' muttered Stan Burrell disconsolately. 'We've made a devil of a mess of it. If that girl isn't found alive, there'll be the very deuce of a row among the high-ups!'

It seemed that Burrell's words were grimly significant, for a police messenger came to Tony Montoni's place. He came on a motor-cycle, and handed Detective-Inspector Martinson the message. Martinson read:

'Police-constable F17 found body of girl in riverside alley. Death caused by knife. Time: 10-13 p.m. Requires identification.'

7

Linda has Visitors

Martinson left Burrell at Montoni's nightclub. Ted Delaney took Jim over to Police Headquarters in his car and then, when Martinson snatched a few seconds reading of the report, they left for the riverside alley.

It was the usual dreary cul-de-sac between tall, soot-stained buildings. The ambulance had been there a few minutes before Jim arrived. A detective from Headquarters had taken some photographs. Martinson gave the scene a quick, grim examination. The dead girl was Elsa Mawn, and she had been stabbed in the back. The weapon had been wrenched away. Martinson, aided by Ted Delaney, the detective and a constable, made a thorough search of the entire cul-de-sac for the missing weapon or, indeed, any other clue however slight. From the blind end of the alley to the quayside the four men searched by the light of powerful electric hand torches borrowed from the ambulance. Beyond establishing the fact that a car had driven into the alley, they found nothing else. The car tyre marks were clearly marked at one part of the gutter where the wheels had passed over some rubbish.

The Big Feller had acted again. This was the third murder. Why had Elsa Mawn been killed?

Soon, commencing tomorrow with Jean Hallinson, there would be a series of inquests. Lem's body would be recovered. The newspapers would turn the grim business into a big story. Jim climbed into Ted's car feeling that the Big Feller had not finished yet.

They returned to Montoni's place, and Jim Martinson walked along to Montoni's office. He left Ted watching the dancers and tasting the whisky offered at the chromium bar.

Martinson felt curious to hear Montoni's answers to questions concerning Mr. Edmund Falconer.

When Jim was admitted to the luxurious office he found Tony Montoni had a visitor. Jim found himself looking into the dark, penetrating eyes of Mrs. Pelham. No one else was in the extravagant office. Jim murmured: 'Good evening, Mrs. Pelham.'

Marian Pelham's firm lips curled in a slight smile.

'Perhaps I should go if you have business to talk?' She turned to Montoni.

'No. Please don't go,' said Martinson. 'I intended to ask Montoni a few questions about Edmund Falconer, and as you are mutual friends, perhaps you could help me.'

Montoni grinned.

'Is Edmund in trouble, Inspector?' He waved his hands. 'And what about my girl singer?'

'She is dead,' said Martinson. 'Murdered. Someone was waiting for her and when she left this building for a few moments they got her, took her away in a car probably. Now this murder is one of a series, and the instigator is an individual whom I call the Big Feller. This person employs underlings sometimes and seems to be able to command a number of riverside cut-throats and other criminals. For example one was clever enough to make up his disguise to resemble you, Montoni. If you had not an alibi for that precise time, it would have been awkward for you. Now Falconer was seen by me today taking a man called Lem Dallas down the river in a launch. Later I saw Lem dead. He had been murdered in cold blood. I don't know why, and I don't know if Falconer was the actual murderer, but, anyway, he is definitely implicated.'

Montoni puffed out his cheeks before replying. 'So that is my friend, Edmund? Ah! But I have so many friends and they are always in trouble. When they are in trouble I try to forget them.'

'Can you tell me where Falconer lived?' asked Martinson. 'How did he earn a living? Who is he?'

Montoni was vague. He spread his hands. 'I do not know. We played cards in my office — he was amusing — I do not ask questions. He was my friend, but I know nothing about him!'

'Did you play with a green dragon pack?'

Montoni grinned hugely. 'Aha! Your detective man ask about the green dragon cards. Yes. We often play — for silly stakes, Inspector!'

'And Mrs. Pelham, have you often played cards with Falconer?' asked Martinson.

'Yes. Just as Tony says,' said Marian Pelham coolly.

'Could you add anything to Montoni's rather vague description of Falconer's activities?'

'It sounds silly, but I can't. I suppose our acquaintanceship was rather superficial,' she smiled. Martinson thought she was a statuesque woman, with her cool, controlled air and her dark intelligent eyes. She looked as capable as a man, he thought. Then she said: 'Don't you think Falconer is this Big Feller person you mention — this riverside master criminal?'

'I have wondered about that,' said Jim Martinson slowly, 'but somehow I think

Falconer is not the Big Feller. He seemed to be just a shade too open with friend Lem. No one would trust Lem Dallas so much as that. So it follows Falconer is in the employ of the Big Feller.'

Marian Pelham brought out a cigarette case. It was a small exquisite gold container. She offered her cigarettes with the assured air of an equal. Then: 'Of course all this about Edmund Falconer is slightly incredible to me. You say he went down the river with a man called Lem Dallas and that later Lem was found dead?'

'Yes.'

She smiled. 'You are leaving a lot of details to the imagination, Inspector. But how do the details prove to you that Edmund Falconer is connected with this Big Feller?'

'Well, Lem was definitely working for the Big Feller. I've known that long before Jean Hallison was murdered. In any case, an attempt was made to kill me, and I think it is a good guess that only the Big Feller would dare to go to that extreme.'

'Are you joking?'

'Not at all,' said Martinson seriously. 'I may say, Mrs. Pelham, that murder is a grave crime, but murder of a policeman in the course of his duty usually brings a hundred percent effort to track the murderer. Few criminals like to risk that. That's why I believe the Big Feller tried to get rid of me, with Falconer helping.'

She exhaled smoke. Martinson thought he saw a trace of admiration in her eyes. He knew she had assessed his height with the appreciation of a tall woman towards a tall man. Martinson swallowed and said hurriedly: 'So you can't give me any real information about Falconer?'

Montoni shook his head. 'So sorry, Inspector. You know, my mind — it is thinking all the time of that poor girl. Why was she killed?'

'I'm not quite sure,' said Martinson. He buttoned his coat. 'When Jean Hallison was murdered the Big Feller 'phoned me hinting that there would be others like her. Then June Carlow and Elsa Mawn were attacked and doped. I believe the Big Feller wanted to question them. Now why? Because there was something he wanted to know. Now Elsa is dead. Lem is dead. I should think Lem was killed because he got in bad with the Big Feller, but Elsa surely did not know the criminal?'

Marian Pelham was following his reasoning carefully.

'I read the account of Jean Hallison's murder in the paper. I should say there is a madman about.'

Jim Martinson looked down at Montoni's dark hair and the man's flashing black eyes. Jim's eyes narrowed.

Montoni and Mrs. Pelham knew Edmund Falconer, and until science perfected some instrument it would always be difficult to know when a person was lying.

'The Big Feller is as sane — as us,' said Jim slowly. 'In confidence I may say I believe the Big Feller is seeking something which he imagines is possessed by one of four girls. Two girls are now dead. June Carlow and Linda Davies remain. It's impossible to guess what this secret may be — I just don't know — but I think Linda Davies has the secret, though she does not realise it. After all, she lived with Jean Hallison. Jean was the first to be attacked.'

'Sometimes I wish I had been a man,' exclaimed Marian Pelham. 'I find your theories quite absorbing, Inspector. I wish I was a detective.'

Montoni laughed loudly. Martinson smiled, and went to the door.

'I'll run along. Your other singer will be sent home with a police escort, Montoni. We must take no chances.'

As Martinson closed the office door and walked along the passage, he wondered if the hint concerning Linda Davies would reach Edmund Falconer and then the Big Feller.

He hoped it would because then the Big Feller could be led to walk into a trap.

Jim found Ted Delaney having his second drink.

'Leave that stuff. We're going over to Moor Park Flats, and for heaven's sake don't let that whisky induce you to take risks. We might both get a stiff fine.'

Ted protested all the way to his car,

and as they climbed in, Jim waved to Detective-Sergeant Burrell.

'I'm going over to interview Miss Davies,' he called out.

Burrell smiled at the departing car.

Jim Martinson found Linda at home in her flat. She had been reading a novel, he noticed as he entered the tiny drawing room with Ted. Linda had laid aside the book. As the men entered, she switched on the main light and turned off the small reading lamp.

'Linda, I've brought Ted Delaney because he has a fast car.'

He made the introduction in a formal manner.

'Linda, I hate to say it, but Elsa Mawn — ' he broke off, and her clear eyes looked up to him in sudden fear. 'She's dead, Linda,' he concluded gently.

She stood still, her face paling slightly. She made no nervous movements with her hands, but Jim knew she was shocked.

'I'd better tell you that Lem Dallas is also dead,' said Jim, 'I've had quite an evening.' And he gave her an account of the fight on the river, the discovery of

Lem's body and then the call to Montoni's place to learn that Elsa Mawn had fallen a victim to the Big Feller.

While he spoke, he was increasingly aware of her desirable face and figure. If she had breeding, she was also a girl in whom there would be a splendid capacity for love. He had met her twice, but it was amazing to realise he had fallen head over heels in love. Her eyes held a light that puzzled him while he was talking to her. Even as he talked of Lem and the Big Feller, another part of his brain was thinking about Linda. What was that light in her eyes? Was she glad to see him again?

Few people can look into another's eyes without seeing expressions that the tongue is reluctant to find words for. There was something in Linda's eyes, but Jim could not define it. He wondered if his own eyes betrayed him. He supposed they did. Linda would know without the necessity for words.

He concluded his brief story. Linda said:

'The Big Feller — as you call him, Jim

— must be mad. Why should Elsa be killed?'

'I've got a theory that the Big Feller is after a secret. What else can it be? Remember, there have been attacks on three girls. The fatal attack on Elsa was the second. Now you will be next.'

'Do you think so?' Linda's voice was low.

'Yes. You will be next if the Big Feller hears the words I spoke in Montoni's office.'

He caught her arm gently, stared at her for a moment. She seemed tall, cool, exquisite. She was wearing a lovely tunic suit that had an air of utter simplicity. Her hair was shaped in a sophisticated coiffure, revealing her shapely ears with delicate pearl earrings that added so much to her poise.

'I'm glad I'm being offered as bait,' she said in the same low voice.

'I wouldn't let the Big Feller touch a hair of your head,' said Jim grimly. 'I dropped the hint about you in Montoni's office because I want to get the Big Feller. But you will have to leave this flat Linda.

We'll get another girl to stay here. She will resemble you greatly — especially with a little make-up — but she will actually be a policewoman. Now if the Big Feller comes here, or sends an underling of his we'll be ready.'

'What if the Big Feller should appear now?' asked Ted Delaney.

Martinson cocked his head to him. 'Well, that will be quick work. The word has to travel to Falconer. It may never reach him or the Big Feller. Montoni and Mrs. Pelham may not see Falconer again, or, if they have some method of communication, they might not bother to get in touch with him. It is all rather vague, but these tricks are worth trying. It might come off.'

'What did you say to Montoni?' asked Linda.

'I said you possessed some secret which the Big Feller is after, though you do not know the details of the secret.'

Linda laughed. 'Sounds rather vague.'

'Perhaps it is, but I believe it to be true. There is something which you or June Carlow possess or know, and the Big

Feller is ready to commit murder for this something.'

Linda was bewildered. 'But I have no secret which belongs to the Big Feller.'

Jim Martinson rubbed his chin. 'Perhaps not. But perhaps the Big Feller thinks you have. Perhaps the Big Feller thinks June Carlow might have the secret or whatever it is, but I've tried to hint that you were the logical one.'

Linda smiled slightly.

'The real reason is because I've made arrangements for you to leave the flat for the next day or so and instal the policewoman who resembles you,' said Jim quickly.

'Well, when do I start moving?'

Jim smiled. 'Now. We shall leave in Ted's Riley, and some time later a girl who looks like you will return in Ted's Riley. If by any remote chance there is a spy around, then it will appear you have returned to your flat. Actually you will be on the other side of the town in a safe little hotel.'

'I shall have to pack,' said Linda firmly. 'I cannot just walk out.'

'So I drive back a policewoman who looks like Linda,' said Ted in a hoarse whisper, when Linda turned into another room to pack. 'That sounds good. Just as well I put this new suit on tonight.'

A sudden ringing came from the flat doorbell. When Linda opened the door two persons smiled at her.

They were Tony Montoni and Marian Pelham. Behind them stood two large policemen.

8

The Crash

Jim Martinson stepped swiftly to the door. 'Come right in, Mrs. Pelham. And Montoni! This is an unexpected visit.'

Jim ushered them into the drawing room, and nodded to the policemen. The two men in uniform guessed that they had to return to their job of standing guard outside.

Martinson introduced Linda to the older woman.

'I'm so sorry to hear about your poor friend, Jean Hallison,' said Marian Pelham. Her dark eyes held Linda's. The girl sensed the strong personality of the other woman. But she thought Marian Pelham was not really sorry about Jean. But then, of course, why should she be? She had never met Jean.

Ted Delaney was introduced to the visitors, and then Jim Martinson asked bluntly: 'Have you some news for me, Montoni?'

Tony Montoni's thick red lips parted in a wide smile. 'So you guess? Yes, we come to tell you things about Mr. Falconer. I talk it over with Marion when you leave. We both agree that there are things you should know, Inspector. We are verree sorry that we did not speak of these things before.'

Martinson nodded quickly. 'So you learned from Burrell that I had left for this flat?'

Marian Pelham spoke impatiently. 'Yes. We've been fools. Montoni and I know that Falconer has a hideout down the river — a place called River House. Have you heard of it?'

Martinson thought quickly.

'A little. But then there are a thousand dumps up and down the river which I have heard about but which take a lifetime to investigate. How do you know that is Falconer's hideout?'

Marian Pelham shot a quick glance at Montoni.

'Falconer told Tony at some time — at least that is what Tony says.'

'Did Falconer state that River House was his hideout?' asked Martinson. 'Why should he tell you that?'

'He was a little drunk one night,' Montoni smiled, showing his superb teeth. 'He say if I ever wanted to find him I should go to River House. But I do not go. Oh, no. Montoni very careful.'

'Why didn't you tell me this when I questioned you?'

'Well, Falconer was our friend. We think we try to help him.' Tony Montoni made a vague Latin gesture. 'But later we know that is wrong. We should help the police.'

'A sudden change of front, eh?' said Martinson unpleasantly. 'Whose idea was it to dash over here?'

At Martinson's blunt tones, Montoni's face assumed a poker expression.

'We thought you'd like to know,' said Marian Pelham coolly. 'As a matter of fact, I encouraged Tony to come over.'

Jim smiled slightly.

'I have to thank you. But you could have given the information to Detective-Sergeant Burrell. Well, we'll have to act on that.'

His words held a note of dismissal in

them. Everyone smiled politely and the two visitors moved to the door.

After a few pleasant 'Good nights' the door closed. Martinson turned to Ted and Linda.

'Now that was very accommodating of our friends. Still, Montoni always was a queer bird.' He turned to Linda's 'phone and rang up Montoni's under manager at the nightclub. He found that Detective-Sergeant Burrell had left the place. Jim 'phoned through to Police Headquarters and found his sergeant there.

'Stan, I've got a job for you. You need some men and possibly the help of the River Police. Get down to River House and surround the place. You might find Edmund Falconer there. He's the chap who slugged me on the head early this evening. I might find time to trot along later. I don't know much about River House except that it is a tall, dilapidated building standing on the very edge of the river near to Black Rock Bend. It's another of these derelict buildings with basements flooded by the river.'

Jim turned to the others with a grin. 'If

a policeman is hampered by red tape, at least he can call on dozens of helping hands. Now I think we'll still carry out our plan of swapping Linda with her almost-double. You know, I thought Montoni and Mrs. Pelham would try to give Falconer the gist of my hint about Linda unknowingly possessing some secret which Falconer's boss would like to get hold of, but it hasn't turned out that way. Still, I'm taking no chances. The Big Feller is clever. If we have a policewoman in this flat, I'll be happier.'

Linda had packed. Her suitcase was lying in a corner of the room. While Martinson had been using the 'phone, she had quickly completed her packing.

They left the flat, and after Linda turned the lock she handed the key to Martinson. They went down to Ted's car.

They climbed into the car, Ted at the wheel and Jim elected to sit with Linda in the delightfully intimate confine of the rear seat. Ted started the engine, and the car slid smoothly away from the kerb.

Its progress was watched by two men sitting inside the dark interior of a saloon

114

car, which lay a good block away from the entrance of the flats.

One man sat at the wheel. He was Edmund Falconer, the very man Martinson sought. His smooth face was fixed in hard, unpleasant lines. His usually urbane eyes were burning with vicious thoughts.

The other man was tall and bulky. He had no hat and his thick black hair grew in long sideboards. His lips were thick, red. His cheeks were large. His black eyes glinted in extraordinary fashion as he looked at the disappearing car.

Falconer eased the clutch of his car. As the vehicle moved swiftly down the road, he shot a glance at his companion. He chuckled grimly.

'This is it. This is where we put on a flaming, dangerous act.' He chuckled again. 'Very dangerous — Montoni. Eh — Montoni?' The other chuckled with him.

★ ★ ★

Jim Martinson planned to send Linda over to the safe little hotel in the West

End of the town. Then Ted and he could pick up the policewoman at Headquarters and bring her back to Linda's flat. After that a trip down the river to River House would be a good idea.

Framcastle boasted a large moor, which skirted one side of the town. The road ran along this showpiece for nearly half a mile. Ted was driving gently along the road — somehow he guessed that Jim Martinson would not thank him for cutting minutes off this journey — when he became aware of the car tearing up behind him.

There wasn't much unusual in that. One or two cars had passed him already, though the road was not very busy. Ted closed to the kerb slightly to allow the speed merchant to pass. A long avenue of unrailed trees skirted the side of the road, forming a boundary to the moor.

The overtaking car came abreast. The driver slowed the vehicle. Ted glanced sideways, fingers light on the wheel, his foot on the accelerator.

The next second's events arose out of Ted's intuition as a born driver.

The driver of the other car pulled at his steering wheel. Ted caught a lightning glimpse of the action and instinctively his foot pressed hard on the accelerator. The other car swung in, pressing Ted's car to the kerb. Ted felt the sudden powerful surge of the engine impelling the car into a swift, sustained leap forward.

But it seemed impossible to avoid a collision with the unrailed trees. Already the left side wheels were running on the kerb. Ted saw a lamp standard looming up. He pressed every ounce out of his engine.

He beat the other car in a fight that had lasted only seconds. Ted's car seemed to heave itself out of the trap. Ted swung the wheel and flung the car off the kerb, missing the lamp standard by an inch.

He felt the right side of the car scrape the other saloon. Then the engine pulled the car clear in a masterful fashion Ted let her tear into the lead.

Ted's elation at avoiding the trap was short-lived. He was watching the speedometer steadily moving up to fifty-five and then on to sixty when a succession of shots cracked above the hum of the engine.

He knew revolver shots when he heard them. He heard Jim Martinson shout: 'They're shooting at the tyres!'

The next moment the car swerved uncontrollably. Ted jerked the wheel right and left, attempting to check its mad impulse to fling itself at the line of trees. Shots were still cracking through the air. Then another tyre punctured with a loud retort.

Ted felt his car leap, even as he desperately trod on the brake. For a few seconds, as the car began to scream under suddenly applied brakes, he thought he had control. Then with a mad leap the car hurtled for the pavement. Ted tried to correct the swerve, but he was a second too late.

The car crashed over the pavement and ran into the boundary of trees that stood two and three deep. A ghastly tearing sound filled the air as the car body dug into the solid tree trunk.

Ted never knew how to describe the next few seconds. It seemed that his brain registered a confused medley of crashing noises, blinding lights and then a dazed stumbling from out of the wreckage.

He was still dazed when two men jumped out of a car that pulled up with a harsh grating of brakes. Ted watched them stupidly. Somehow the gun which one carried held no significance to his dazed mind.

One of the men wrenched the door of the wrecked car open. He ducked his head inside the rear compartment, and a moment later dragged out the girl.

The fog was clearing from Ted's brain. He lunged towards the man who had Linda over his shoulder. Even as Ted moved forward, Jim Martinson crawled slowly from the wreck.

Martinson stared into the face of Montoni. Martinson's vision was hazy, but he knew he was gazing at Montoni. He couldn't understand it.

'Should I let these blokes have it?' asked Edmund Falconer.

His companion had no time to answer. The sound of an approaching car came to their ears, and then the sound as the car braked suddenly to a standstill.

'Come on. Let's get out of this,' snapped the big Latin in a sudden spasm of alarm.

Falconer seemed to be suddenly infected with the other's alarm. They dived for their car. The big Latin was carrying Linda. She seemed to be unconscious. Martinson ran after them, almost stumbling as a number of painful lights shot across his eyes.

The car that had just arrived had stopped ten yards away. A door clanged as the owner got out. The sound coincided with the sudden snarl of an engine as Falconer and his companion made a getaway.

By the time Ted and Jim stumbled over to the kerb, the saloon was tearing down the road. The man who had just arrived stared open-mouthed at the departing car. He had seen the big man carrying the girl, and he could not understand what was going on.

'I say, is he running away? Hell, you've had an awful crash!'

'I'm a police officer,' said Martinson.

'Here is my warrant. We've got to stop that car.' Jim clenched his hands as the middle-aged car driver peered at the papers Jim had thrust at him. Martinson turned to Ted. 'Did you see — Montoni?'

'He's the Big Feller!' retorted Ted.

'Is he? Why did he bother to come over to tell me that Falconer could be found hiding at the River House?'

The middle-aged car driver murmured: 'Amazing.'

'Let me have your car,' said Jim Martinson. He did not wait for an answer. The other saloon had disappeared. But Martinson guessed it would be hurtling down the moor road. He grabbed Ted's arm, and they jumped into the new car. 'Are you coming, sir?' shouted Martinson.

The man shook his head vigorously.

Ted's feet found the clutch and accelerator by instinct and an expert knowledge of cars. Within a second the car was drawing away from the scene of the wreck, leaving an astounded gentleman surveying the road and the sadly damaged car among the trees.

'We'll try not to damage his car,' muttered Martinson. 'But we've simply got to commandeer it. Ted, the Big Feller means to get Linda.'

'What the devil is the reason for it?'

'I tell you,' said Martinson, 'he is after some secret. It is my opinion — and I'm making a long guess — that this secret doesn't really exist.'

'But the Big Feller thinks it does,' commented Ted.

'Exactly.'

9

'I Will Kill You!'

Ted Delaney drove the car at its utmost speed. The wheels zipped across tarmacadam, and the moor was lost to view. Ted guessed that the other saloon had gained no more than a quarter mile, and the car he was driving gave promise of eating that distance in seconds. He drove grimly, conscious that he ached in every limb. It was an absolute miracle that they had emerged from the wreckage of his car without broken bones.

Martinson was thinking on those lines, too, for he suddenly said: 'I hope Linda suffered no harm in the crash. We were deuced lucky. You handled your car splendidly, Ted.'

Ted smiled grimly. 'Perhaps. But I've torn my new suit.'

Jim Martinson said quickly: 'There they are! I swear that's their car in the distance!'

Ted had driven like fury for a mile, with a speedometer indicating seventy-five miles an hour. With a grim chuckle he wondered if the old gentleman had ever driven his car at that speed before.

Disregarding the fact that he was in a built-up area, Ted raced through the main street, came up behind the saloon.

He was closing to about fifty yards when the other car accelerated.

'He's seen us,' stated Jim. 'They haven't been driving full out. Perhaps they thought neither of us were fit to drive.'

Ted grimly hoped the pain in his back was no more than a bruise. Possibly it wasn't. But it hurt like blazes, all the same.

The next twenty minutes were crazy times for Ted. He had never driven a car before with complete disregard for all traffic rules and road signs, but he was forced to do so in order to hang on to the trail of the other car.

If Falconer was driving the saloon, he was an expert motorist or, perhaps, desperate. Several pedestrians nearly lost their lives as the two cars, sometimes merely yards separating them, hurtled round street corners, diving with engines racing into side streets.

On one straight road Ted could have overtaken the other car and possibly repeated Falconer's previous tactics and forced them to crash, but he dared not risk it with Linda in the other car.

Several times Falconer's saloon gained a lead by skidding dangerously round unexpected side streets. But Ted never lost him. Police whistles frequently pierced the night air. Once a white-gloved policeman nearly got knocked down as he made a futile effort to hold up Falconer's car.

The chase went on through the city and down to the narrow riverside streets. If Falconer hoped to shake Ted off in these incredible streets, he underrated the man on his track.

Ted sent the car speeding through dark narrow alleys where an obstacle would have meant disaster. Sometimes he had to waste a valuable second discovering that Falconer had surged up the street parallel with the one they had just rushed down.

Martinson guessed that the whole of Framcastle police patrol cars would now be alert for the two desperately driven cars that had plunged through the city streets. But so far Falconer had had the devil's luck. Ted and Jim were the only ones on his trail.

Ted drove at high speed along a cobbled alley in pursuit of the other car. He saw the taillight turn the distant corner. A few seconds later, after a bumpy plunge down the narrow thoroughfare, he rounded the corner. His car nearly smashed into the stationary saloon.

Martinson saw the two men jumping out. One was carrying Linda. They ran to the door of a derelict building, which stood with its foundations in the river. A grimy shop window stretched the length of the ground floor, with the gable end dropping into the water. It was a typical sample of the dilapidated type of building, which decorated many parts of the riverside. What it had been designed for and for what purpose it was now used, no one could tell.

Martinson caught the man carrying

Linda before he could open the dark door. Martinson grabbed him. The man let the girl fall, and as she fell she moaned slightly. Jim gave him a wicked uppercut that nearly killed the man, and when his murderous feeling had passed he saw he was attacking 'Montoni'.

The man's disguise was now apparent. True he was Montoni's height and his black hair was typically Latin, but his features, though heavy and fleshy like Montoni's, were not a true double. Jim saw him clearly, and not dazedly as had been the case after climbing from Ted's wrecked car.

Ted Delaney had grabbed Falconer. Ted was no slouch in a rough-house, and he slammed the other man furiously. Ted was thinking of Linda — and perhaps of his wrecked car.

Martinson paused in his job of half-killing Montoni's double.

'Where's your boss? Here?'

The man did not reply. Martinson gave him some more punishment. The man began to sob and then words jerked from him.

'You swine — leave me alone!'

Martinson rammed his fist into the other's face remorselessly. The man cried: 'I'll tell you!'

'Where is your boss? Who is he?'

'I don't know him. Only Falconer is in plush with the boss. You'll find the boss upstairs.'

Martinson felled the man deliberately. He stooped, picked up Linda and carried her towards the car. He called out to Ted. 'Look after her, will you, Ted? I'm going in there.'

Ted Delaney had knocked Falconer to the ground. The man was semi-conscious, and should prove no trouble.

Martinson crashed his big frame against the door, and after only two blows the structure gave. The door opened somewhat crazily after Jim's treatment. He went up some stairs feeling in an ugly mood.

He saw a light flicker for a second from the top of the stairs, and then the yellow gleam was snapped out. Martinson went up the stairs softly, two at a time.

He came to a door at the top of the landing. He stood listening for a tense moment. He guessed that this was the door that had shown the momentary light. The remainder of the ramshackle building seemed deserted. Jim suddenly heard a slight noise as if someone had walked gently over creaky floorboards.

Without hesitation he tried the door. It was locked. He smiled grimly at this evidence of human activity. He stepped back softly for two yards, and then ran at the door.

It was not built for rough treatment and promptly burst open.

Martinson checked his headlong rush. He stood in a room that was totally dark. He stood tense, because he knew there was someone else in the room. Nothing tangible could be seen in the all-embracing velvety darkness. But he knew someone was there.

Then a voice said: 'So you've found me Inspector?'

Martinson said gently: 'Yes. And I know who you are.'

'Indeed.'

'Yes, you were very anxious to contact Linda after I hinted she unwittingly possessed your secret. So anxious you sacrificed your River House, but not Edmund Falconer.'

In the pause that followed his words, they both heard the whine of car engines racing up the waterfront. They were unmistakably police cars.

'Better come quietly,' said Jim. 'The police have arrived. Your henchmen's mad dash through town has stirred up the whole patrol.'

'I will kill you, Martinson!'

He dropped to the floor swift as a falling stone, but softly as a feather.

A shot rang out above his head.

He lay, not daring to breath. He wondered if she could see him or an outline of him in the gloom.

And then a voice said: 'I will kill you.'

He lay, waiting. A few strained seconds ticked like ominous steps to the gallows. The voice said again: 'I will kill you.'

Martinson wondered at the queer mechanical tone. Another second and a sudden noise impelled him to raise his head.

At the end of the room a window was

being raised by Marian Pelham. Even as Martinson raised his head sounds of feet clumping up the stairs of the old building came to his ears. The police were coming to investigate.

Martinson raised himself. He was in time to see Marian Pelham climb through the window and leap out into space.

It dawned upon him in grim, ugly thoughts that she had leaped from the gable end into the deep muddy river.

He ran to the window. He looked out, seeing nothing but the dull swirl of filthy water.

Then the police came in.

* * *

Detective-Inspector Jim Martinson came over to Linda as she sat on the small settee. A small electric fire burned brightly but spuriously, for Linda's flat did not need the heat. Jim glanced down at her hair, thought it fragrant and soft.

'Thank goodness you did not break any bones in that car crash,' he murmured. 'I'd marry you even if I had to wheel you to church, but all the same I like to see you whole.'

She smiled at his earnestness. 'I wish you'd get on telling me about Marian Pelham.'

'Righto. Can I kiss you then?'

'I should expect it, my dear.'

He kissed her, long and hungrily there and then. He seemed to gain his confidence, and continued.

'As I was saying, Marian Pelham was an extraordinary woman. She ought to have been born a man, for it seems she yearned for power. She had a shrewd business sense, if everything Falconer tells me is true. Now Jean Hallison found out her identity through playing around with Lem Dallas. Lem got drunk one night — more than usually tight. He gave Jean a strong hint. He probably thought he could dispose of the girl at any moment. But Jean was shrewd. She had always longed for money. This seemed to be her chance.

'She got money all right after meeting the Big Feller. Jean uncovered Marian Pelham's private address and went there.

Jean began to blackmail Marian Pelham. She received the money through Lem for a period, and this was the money Jean told you she had inherited.

'Of course, there came the night when Marian Pelham decided to kill Jean, not because of the small sums she was extracting but because the girl was dangerous alive. So she was kidnapped and killed.

'Then Lem met his fate in the river. He was stabbed by Edmund Falconer at the instructions of the Big Feller. Lem, it was decided, had betrayed Marian Pelham by talking to Jean. Marian had not taken vengeance earlier because she always planned to get Jean through Lem somehow.

'Falconer tells me that before Jean Hallison was murdered, she spoke of a tiny rice-paper note she had wedged into the back of a locket belonging to one of her girl friends. Right now all sorts of girls are wearing these little gold lockets. It's a craze as you know, Linda. This note was Jean's fluffy-headed idea of insurance against the big shot she was blackmailing.

No one knew about the tiny scrap of note except Jean, but it was her silly idea the note would be found sooner or later. If the note was found while Jean was still in a safe position, then Jean intended to explain it was just one big joke. Of course, Jean could have left a letter — that's the usual sort of cover — but I think she felt she could not exactly trust her girl friends not to look at the letter.

'She did not want her friends finding out she got her money by blackmail. So the rice-paper note in the little gold locket was her pet idea. Mind you this is the way I build it up, judging from the facts Falconer has told me. But Jean must have convinced Marian, because it explains the dope attacks on June and Elsa. The thug who impersonated Montoni, was to kidnap the girls if they were not wearing their lockets. By kidnapping they could be made to divulge exact information for getting the locket or lockets in the quickest possible time without raising suspicion as to what was being sought. Marian Pelham could not just risk ignoring the existence of the locket on the chance that it might be lost, or the note never found. And Jean's little idea did not protect her. She was murdered just the same.'

Linda rose on a sudden impulse and went to a dressing table in her bedroom. She returned with an attractive little gold locket on a chain.

'A lot of girls are wearing these,' she said. 'It's the only one I've got . . . '

Martinson nicked it open. He took the back out, but there was no scrap of paper.

'Has June Carlow a locket?' he asked.

Linda considered. 'Yes, I think so.'

'The note can only be in her locket because Elsa Mawn was killed after Marian Pelham had collected the girl's locket.

'Linda, I dropped a hint about you having something hidden in your flat and you unaware of it. Perhaps I used vaguer terms, but Marian Pelham read it that way. So she came over to contact you on the excuse of giving me information about River House and Falconer. Before she left Montoni's club, she had 'phoned Falconer telling him to quit River House.

The place was used mostly as a hideout for her yacht. Falconer was told to go to Moor Park Flats and bring Montoni's double.

'Marian Pelham had persuaded Montoni that it was his duty to tell me about Falconer. It was true that Falconer had told Montoni once that he could be found at River House. Falconer was Marian Pelham's trusted lieutenant, and in the end the only one who knew that the Big Feller was a woman and leader of a racket that stretched all the way down the river. And I suppose, Linda, she wanted to see if you were wearing a little gold locket.'

'It was in my drawer,' said Linda. 'But even so — no note! Poor Jean's silly little trick!'

Linda stared at the fire. Jim slowly placed an arm round her slim waist.

'I haven't rushed you like some silly ass — I hope,' he said anxiously.

Her reply thrilled him.

'My dear this was inevitable from the moment we met. I knew that long ago, and that was when you came to the door of this flat and asked if I was ill.'

'Sounds dammed silly now,' he grinned. 'I've an idea — Let's start all over again. No murders — no horrors — just a great romance for we two. I'll go out of the flat and ring the bell again. You open the door, think of something to say and I'll promise not to ask if you are ill.'

He went out. He lit a cigarette, pressed the bell. Linda opened the door, and her face was radiant with an expectant smile.

'Hello,' said Jim Martinson.

'Come right in, darling,' she said.

CASE OF THE
WAYWARD BROTHER

1

Vicious Murder

Tim Ryan was walking slowly past Cellini's nightclub in Soho when the tinkle of glass and the crash of opening doors made him pause. In the darkish deserted street Ryan's cigarette stub glowed. He took it from his mouth and shielded it with his cupped hand. Then he stepped back into a convenient doorway.

From a low basement door of the nightclub a man dashed into the street like a wild animal. As he passed under an adjacent lamp standard Ryan saw his coat was half-ripped from his back and that blood streamed from a wound in his head. He had scarcely run five yards when another man lurched from the nightclub door. The pursuer raised a revolver and fired point-blank at the running man. The man sprawled to the pavement, and then bullet after bullet ripped into his body until the magazine of the gun was empty. Ryan drew in his breath sharply. As a private investigator he had seen samples of brutality, but this vicious murder sickened even him. Here was gang warfare happening in the heart of London.

A police whistle blew in the distance, and then from the nightclub door a girl dashed past the murderer and ran like a hunted creature: She was young, alert and apparently crazed with fear, for she almost fell in her wild haste. The man with the gun raised his weapon. A second later he remembered the magazine was empty, thrust the gun into his pocket and started chasing the girl,

Tim Ryan threw away his cigarette, and his lithe body strained forward. Although he was a good many yards behind the girl and the murderer, he ran with incredibly long, silent strides and made up the distance. Even so the killer caught the girl before Ryan. The man's hands went round the girl's throat. Tim Ryan leaped the last six yards. His hard, bunched fist slammed wickedly into the murderer's thick neck. The man gave a grunt and, as his hands left the girl's throat, he wheeled. Ryan caught the glint of an ugly knuckle-duster as the man's fists jerked towards his face. Ryan ducked with the skill of a born boxer. He stepped back to adjust the range to his opponent who was bundling closely to him, and then Ryan let the man have it. A powerful uppercut followed a left hook and the man sagged drunkenly.

Ryan saw that he was a vicious-looking specimen with a scarred face, and high cheekbones. He lay slumped grotesquely on the pavement. Tim Ryan caught the girl's hand. She stood against some railings, striving to control her choked breathing. Ryan got a photographic-glimpse of blonde hair, a sophisticated, intelligent face and vivid, generous lips.

'Get me away,' she gasped. 'Quick — before the police come!' She looked at him beseechingly.

He reflected swiftly. His citizen's duty was to stay until the police arrived, to give a statement about what he had witnessed. He glanced down at the unmoving figure.

The murderer wasn't going anywhere in a hurry.

There had almost certainly been other witnesses to the shooting, and the police would easily link the man's gun — still in his pocket — to his victim.

Impulsively, he grabbed her arm and started to run her along the street.

People were appearing from doorways and from the main street to gape curiously at Cellini's nightclub. Tim Ryan passed some of the gapers before he took a short cut through another club premises. He urged the girl along a passage, avoided the main rooms and came out of the front entrance. They were in Salop Street — one street away from Cellini's. Ryan turned to take stock of the girl. She looked an intelligent type, but he wanted to hear her speak. He wanted to know what she had been doing in Cellini's club, and why she wanted to avoid the police.

'Why was that murderous thug after you?' he asked.

She paused, sizing him up; she saw, in the well-lighted street, a medium-man in a dark, raglan coat and an individualistic hat. Ryan had a mannish mouth and eyes that never betrayed his thoughts. They were grey eyes, hard but very often human.

'It's not a very pleasant story,' she said.

'Suppose you tell me your story,' said Tim Ryan. 'I might be able to help you. I've just finished a case that brought me fifty guineas a week retainer for doing almost nothing, so I can afford to give some free advice in a good cause.'

The blonde seemed more interested.

'Do you often get fifty guineas a week for doing nothing, Mister — ?'

'My name is Tim Ryan. Ryan Investigations is the full handle. As to the fifty guineas, it was sweet. Many years ago I worked for less in shillings.'

'Success story!' she murmured. 'Local boy makes good. This is fascinating! Tell me more.'

He bit his lip. 'Suppose you tell me.'

'Very well. I expect you'll learn all about me, as you're a detective. My name is Delia Lucas. You might even see me in the illustrated weekly magazines.'

'How come?'

'Well, it has happened,' she said coolly. 'I get around a lot socially and I'm engaged to Peter Arnell, the film star.'

She was serenely confident now. Tim Ryan stared, wondering how old she might be. Perhaps only nineteen, he thought. He began to add things up. She had stuck her nose into Cellini's, coolly thinking she could carry anything off. Maybe she had until things got rough.

'Well, Miss Lucas, now that we know a little about each other, why not tell me about tonight's affair? You said it was a long story. That doesn't sound as if you were accidentally involved in the scuffle.'

She extended her hand to Ryan.

'Thanks for helping me,' she said frankly. 'But, honestly, I prefer to look after myself. Goodnight, and thank you, Mr. Ryan. It isn't often I meet a detective. Sorry — I mean investigator.'

Before he could gather his wits together, she walked away. Tim Ryan lighted a cigarette and saw her disappear round the street corner. Then he resettled his odd-shaped hat on his head and strode off moodily.

Ryan wondered about the man who had been shot dead. Who was he? The girl had not seemed upset about the murder. Therefore, it seemed the man was of no consequence to her, and murder a common event in her young life.

He went into his office, stared at Miss Hudding's typewriter and wondered what his unbeautiful secretary was doing at this hour — probably knitting. Then he went into an adjacent room and started to scan a pile of magazines. They were mostly illustrated magazines. When Ryan finally found a picture of Delia Lucas, the photogravure was well-placed in a shilling weekly. The picture had been taken at some fashionable ball by flashlight camera. Even so, Delia still looked lovely, and her escort could be regarded as equally handsome. Under the photograph was a caption:

'Miss Delia Lucas and Peter Arnell were attractive visitors at the Gainsborough Ball.'

Peter Arnell was tall, dark and handsome. Tim Ryan thought the man perhaps a little too scrupulously groomed, and his smile somewhat complacent.

'Typical film star,' murmured Ryan.

The telephone rang peremptorily, and he crossed to the instrument.

'Hello. Tim Ryan speaking.'

'Mr. Ryan, I'm so glad to find you in. This is Delia Lucas.'

'The devil it is!'

'Listen. I wonder if you will help me after I refused your aid? Mr. Ryan, I find I need someone I can trust. Oh, I can't tell you much over a 'phone! Could you help me for fifty guineas a week?'

'You can have a week of my time free,' said Ryan, eagerly remembering her blonde hair. 'When can you come over?'

'Immediately. I 'phoned only to make sure you were at home.'

She hung up. Ryan went upstairs into his flat and sat waiting the girl's arrival. He smoked two cigarettes feverishly. Then he lay back in the chair luxuriously and let his thoughts wander concerning the girl. At the moment she did not seem quite real, and yet, oddly, she fascinated him. He admitted he was more interested in Delia Lucas than in the possibility of her producing a tough case for him to investigate.

He flung away his third cigarette towards a realistically-glowing electric fire just as the bell rang. He went down the flight of stairs to admit the visitor.

Delia Lucas was still wearing her youthful coat, and she was hatless. Ryan guided her towards a chair, offered cigarettes and produced some sherry.

'I changed my mind about you, Mr. Ryan, when I got home and found Raymond was still on the loose.'

'Raymond?'

'He's my brother and he has been missing for a week. I want to find him. Actually I know he has got himself mixed up with a man called Spider Malan, a man who organises gambling on a huge scale, and Raymond is spending money so quickly that he'll be ruined. But there is more than that even, though I'm only guessing. Spider Malan is a dope agent!'

'Yes, that's so,' he nodded. 'Spider sells Marihuana cigarettes and cocaine to silly people of the upper crust or any crust if they have the money. If Spider has your brother under his wing, it's a bad job.'

'I went to Cellini's tonight with a rat of

a man,' went on the girl quickly. 'For twenty pounds he was going to point out Spider Malan to me. This man's name was Sid Minter and he was a typical night-club hanger-on. I met him at Cellini's.'

'Can't say I know the name,' said Ryan. 'What happened there?'

'Minter was the man who got killed. He ran foul of another man at Cellini's, and I think this other man imagined that Minter was trying to make some money by talking to cops. They started to fight, and I was rather frightened. I managed to retreat to the cloakroom and dash out after I heard the gunshots.'

'And what earthly use would it be to have Spider Malan pointed out to you?' asked Ryan impatiently.

'I don't know. But I was trying to do something — anything to help my brother.'

Ryan looked at her quizzically, considering her typical feminine reasoning. She stared into his eyes calmly. He noticed her eyes were coral blue.

'What about your father?' he asked. 'Why doesn't he get the police on to

Spider Malan — not that the police have anything definite on the man otherwise they'd put him away double-quick.'

'My father is very ill,' she said. 'He is rather old now and no one has told him about Raymond.'

'Old?'

'Well, he's sixty, and he's not very strong.'

'Well, what about the family solicitors? Surely they could contact the police?'

He was determined to drag the truth from her. After all, why shouldn't she call the police who were more able to take action than was a private dick?

'I don't want the police,' she said tensely. 'I've already told you that. Raymond is a fool, and he is three years older than me. If you must know, I can't be sure that he is not mixed up with Spider Malan's criminal activities. I simply want Raymond rescued from Spider's grip without any comeback. Can you help me find Raymond?'

He extracted a revolver from a nearby drawer, and became business-like as he loaded it.

'Yes. We'll start right now, Miss Lucas.'

2

Ryan Pulls a Gun

Tim Ryan sat beside Delia as the taxi travelled through quiet streets. He appreciated her composure. Her father was ill and her brother going the rounds in company with London's notorious Spider Malan, yet she was facing her problems with coolness.

'We're going to Nick Casey's place because Nick and Spider are pretty pally just now,' said Ryan. 'We need somewhere to launch off. God knows how we'll get under the skin of this case.'

She fell silent again. The taxi brought them swiftly to a street in Soho and they alighted. Ryan paid off the driver.

'Now Nick is a shady character,' said Ryan. 'We'll dine and wine and see if he still has that card game in the back room.'

They had to descend basement steps; it was that sort of place. They entered a warm atmosphere where a few couples in evening dress gyrated on a diminutive floor to the strains of a strident quartet. At a chromium bar a tall, weedy man dispensed cocktails at astonishing prices.

'Would you know Spider Malan if you saw him?' Ryan asked..

'I know he is a sinister-looking man,' said Delia promptly. 'But I've yet to see him myself.'

'Spider Malan is tall and very dark,' said Ryan. 'Maybe he is sinister. Spider has long arms and long legs, though his clothes are usually immaculate. Spider must shave twice every day. He has large bluish cheeks and a hefty chin.'

'If only I could see Raymond and talk to him!' exclaimed Delia.

'I think he needs more than a talking,' said Ryan grimly.

The quartet were playing a quickstep number and Tim Ryan leaned towards Delia.

'Now what is the name of that tune?'

'Inevitably it's about love,' she told him.

'That's a universal craze. Would you like to dance?'

'But we're looking for Raymond.' She paused. 'All right, let's dance.'

Ryan discovered the joys of dancing with an angel. Delia moved and talked just the way he always thought a woman should move and talk. He felt he was dancing with a film star.

When they returned to their table, a man, standing beside a palm in a tub, smiled slickly at Tim Ryan. Ryan smiled back.

'That's Nick Casey,' he told Delia. 'Nick will always treat me right because I know some things about him.'

Tim Ryan beckoned to the smiling man. Nick approached with geniality written all over his fat face. He made a large figure in his evening suit.

'Hello, Nick,' Ryan greeted. 'Delia — permit me to introduce Nick Casey. Nick — Miss Lucas. Park it, Nick.'

A chair creaked when Nick placed his weight upon it.

'Ever see Spider Malan these days?' asked Tim Ryan as he offered his cigarettes.

'Sure.'

'D'you know anything about the boy he is taking for a mug?'

Nick's grin faded slowly. He got up.

'You don't want to have anything to do with that, Tim,' he said seriously. 'Spider has a mug, and that's all there is to it. I can't tell you anything.'

'I want to know where the boy is hiding,' said Ryan, business-like.

'You'll have to ask the Spider about that, Tim. I wouldn't know.'

'You know all right,' said Tim Ryan grimly. 'Now where is Spider Malan's mug? Is Spider coming here tonight? Maybe tomorrow night?'

'He isn't coming here tonight, Tim. Take my advice. The Spider is getting wicked. He's got some tough boys round him.'

'Yes, I know. One of them did a murder tonight. He must have been tight or hopped. He mightn't get away with it. Now, Nick, how can I find the Lucas boy?'

Ryan knew Nick Casey was uneasy. The fat man was wishing he had looked the other way when Ryan had smiled at him.

'I want to know, Nick,' said Ryan. 'Quick.'

155

'Look, Tim, you don't want to get mixed up — '

'Have I to talk to Grogan of the Yard, Nick?'

'All right,' said Nick Casey grimly. 'You can have it. The Lucas sucker is with Spider Malan now — where they've been all the week, and that is at Charlotte Hi's place in Chinatown.'

'I've heard of the lady,' murmured Ryan. 'She's some gal!'

Nick looked around him uneasily.

'Look, Tim. Do me a favour. Drink up and leave. If Spider learns I've talked to you I'll be in trouble. He is as clever as the devil.'

When Ryan was outside with Delia he said to her: 'Nick's actually a good sort, but he'll never run straight so long as he owns that nightclub.'

'You've put me on to Raymond's trail, Tim,' she said. Delia was thinking mostly of her brother. Her eyes gleamed up to him and her silky skin was pale in the streetlights.

'I'd do more than that for you, Delia.'

They stepped into the shadows. Tim

Ryan placed his arm round her waist.

She did not resist. Her eyes were still gleaming and her lips were upturned. Whether it was by accident or not, Ryan did not know but what followed seemed as natural as daylight.

He drew her close to him and for a few seconds kissed her hard on the mouth. Then she fought from his grasp with a little cry.

'I actually let you do that,' she gasped. 'I must be mad. I'm engaged to Peter.'

'Where is Peter Arnell tonight?' he asked savagely.

'I don't know. Perhaps he is reading his latest part at his flat. Perhaps he is at his club. Why do you ask?'

'I just wondered.' Ryan halted. 'Look, Delia, I'm going to Charlotte Hi's place now. I don't think you should come along.'

'I don't mind danger.'

'I know. But from what I've heard, Charlotte Hi keeps strange company. I've never met the lady, but I hear she's an Asiatic of sorts with a few other nationalities stirring her hot blood. Now go home, Delia.'

157

'Should I look up Peter?' she asked spitefully.

'I guess you'll do what the deuce you like!' snapped Ryan. 'You're that type.'

A few blocks along the road was a taxi stand; and Tim Ryan placed the protesting girl in a taxi. He got her address after a bit of wrangling — a large block of luxury flats off Bayswater Road.

★ ★ ★

Ryan came to Charlotte's premises and stared up at the dark, dilapidated front. The street was badly lit, as if too much light might show to passers-by the real ugliness of the place. Ryan had jogged his memory to recall everything he knew about the extraordinary woman known as Charlotte Hi. She was part Chinese and part French and goodness knows what other nationalities featured in her ancestry.

Charlotte Hi ostensibly ran a boarding house and restaurant. Ryan strolled past and looked at the restaurant window. It was darkened, and apparently Charlotte

Hi had closed that section of her business for the night. Ryan wondered what was happening behind those grimy windows on the other floors.

Unless Nick was lying, Spider Malan and the Lucas boy were inside that ordinary, grimy building. Perhaps Spider was running his poker games where the stakes mounted tensely.

A lone constable, standing beneath a lamp-standard, was whistling softly to himself when Ryan approached.

'I'm going into Charlotte Hi's place, Jack,' began Ryan. 'I want to come out the way I go in. I might even bring a friend. Now supposing I don't come out after, say, twenty minutes, I'd like some policemen to come in for me. Got that?'

The young constable nodded. Tim Ryan sauntered up to a door and knocked. He had to knock loudly four times before sounds of someone approaching came to his ears. The door opened. Ryan inserted his foot and stared at a scowling, bald-headed man.

'What do you want?'

'Why the devil didn't you open this

door sooner?' snarled Ryan. 'Get out of my way. I'm a pal of Spider Malan. I'm late. I want to see Spider . . . '

'I never seen you before.'

'How long you had this job, curly?'

'Six months,' growled the man suspiciously.

'Out my way,' snarled Ryan. 'I've been inside for a year, That's how you've never seen me.' Tim Ryan lowered his voice, and asked confidentially: 'Where's Spider?'

The confidential note was a trick that had more than once proved successful with the slow-witted. Ryan infused into those two words the suggestion that Spider and he were thick as thieves, and that all arguments were therefore a waste of time.

'Spider's with the mugs, Mister, an' — '

'Lead me to him, curly,' Tim Ryan shouldered his way into a dingy passage and closed the door behind him with an air of confidence which could have been used to sell gold bricks to lawyers. He whispered: 'There's a copper along the road. I don't want him to see me.'

He swung to a door, judging it to be

the one that led to the assembly.

As his left hand gripped the handle, his right hand fondled the gun in his overcoat pocket. After a second's pause, he stepped into the room.

Ryan took a photographic glance of the whole gathering, noting the four tables, the groups of men and women with card hands and stacked wads of paper money lying before them. Ryan's hard eyes searched for the youth he wanted and — by sheer luck — found him immediately. There was no mistaking the resemblance to Delia in the handsome face of a tall youth who glanced up at the opening door. Perhaps there were signs of weakness in his flushed face, but Tim Ryan did not think about that.

Spider Malan was playing at one of the widely separated tables. A limp cigarette hung from his mouth. His black-jowled, saturnine face scowled at the intruder. He rose to his feet.

'Ryan! What do you want?'

'Hey! You ain't no pal of the boss!' jerked the bald man, realisation dawning in his slow mind.

Tim Ryan pulled his gun out and pointed it significantly at the group with whom Spider was playing. He knew instantly he was playing a dangerous game, but there was no other way. His gun covered the other groups of gamblers, and among them was Charlotte Hi, her black eyes staring at him calmly. She was definitely Oriental, and years of cunning and dissipated life were surely leaving their ugly marks on her yellow face. She was medium height, and wore a flowered evening dress, which seemed incongruous among the motley types present. A few of the women were equally well-dressed, but the men wore various clothes, from chalk-striped lounge suits to evening dress, with one individual sporting a silk scarf in place of a collar and tie.

'Some crew!' muttered Ryan, and then aloud: 'Raymond Lucas — I want you. Come here — quick!'

Ryan sensed some movement among the surprised gamblers.

'If you've got guns, keep 'em in your pockets!' he said rapidly. 'One of you might be clever on the draw, but I'll get

Spider sure. Furthermore, I've got cops outside, and if I don't come out in time, they'll come in. You wouldn't like a good night's business spoilt, Spider! You've got some ripe mugs here.'

'Keep calm, folks,' drawled Spider Malan. 'This feller is just a third-rate private dick who likes trouble. He might get it, too. What do you want with Raymond, Mister Ryan?'

'I simply want him. I like his face. Come here, boy, and hurry. This isn't a healthy spot.'

Sarcasm dripped from Tim Ryan's tongue. Raymond Lucas came over slowly and a trifle drunkenly. Ryan had to step sideways cautiously so that the young fellow would not get in his line of fire.

'I'm taking Raymond away, Spider,' said Ryan. 'You'll have to make do with the other mugs.' He eyed the whole scene narrowly. His throat felt slightly dry. He wished to devil he was out of the place. He felt he was walking along a path strewn with boobytraps.

'Get out into the passage!' hissed Ryan to Raymond. 'Hurry. I'm taking you to

Delia. She wants to make a man out of you.'

'Who the devil are you?' demanded Raymond stupidly.

'You utter fool! Get out!' Ryan snarled.

The young man walked past the bald man, muttering angrily. Ryan had seen a scared expression in his eyes. Ryan backed to the door after him, avoiding the doorman who was watching him sullenly a mere four yards distant.

Then at the door Ryan raised his revolver and shot rapidly at the three hanging electric lights. It was a sample of clever marksmanship, but men leaped from the tables towards him, determined to get him.

3

Wild Youth.

Tim Ryan ran along the basement passage towards the staircase, pushing the protesting Raymond Lucas before him, Once Raymond nearly stumbled and Ryan had to haul him to his feet. He cursed and nearly tore the other's coat collar as he wrenched him up.

At the foot of the stairs, Tim Ryan halted. He shouted to Raymond: 'Get up! Get out into the street!'

Then Ryan took a potshot down the passage at the doorman who lumbered from the gambling den door. Two other men, who spilled out from the room, tried to dash madly into adjoining doors in an effort to seek cover. Ryan let loose another shot and then ran up the stairs two at a time. He chuckled grimly to himself. He was near the street door and the episode seemed nearly over. He could congratulate himself upon an audacious stroke, which, by good luck had come off.

He wrenched open the street door and ran into the cool night air. All at once he bumped into two men. One was in uniform, and Ryan recognised the constable as a friend. The other man was Raymond Lucas. He was gripped firmly by the policeman.

'This your pal, sir?'

'That's him.'

'Get him away. I'm going to blow my whistle, and we'll investigate Charlotte Hi's place. That shooting will provide a good excuse.'

'It's a gambling joint and goodness knows what else,' jerked Ryan.

'Don't we know it! But Charlotte is clever. She can clean the place up inside five minutes. Everything and everyone has a bolthole. We can't convict simply because we don't like her face.'

Ryan hurried away, gripping Raymond by the arm. In cold theory, he (Ryan) had broken the peace by using firearms, but he did not wish to argue the theory of this serious crime.

It was some ten minutes later, inside a taxi speeding towards the more exclusive environs of Bayswater Road, that Ryan realised what he suspected about Raymond Lucas was true. Raymond had all the hazy appearance of one who has smoked too many Marihuana cigarettes.

Ryan paid off his taxi near Hyde Park, and decided to walk Raymond along the road to see if fresh air would restore his sense of proportion. That was the effect of Marihuana. The acrid weed made life easier for its addicts by blunting the smoker's perceptions. How on earth Raymond Lucas expected to win at poker in such a haze was difficult to understand. But, no doubt, he had been led on from one cigarette to another all night.

'How much have you lost to Spider?' asked Ryan,

'Mind your own damned business,' drawled Raymond.

Ryan shook the other's arm in disgust.

'Don't you realise your sister has poked her head into rotten dumps trying to find you? And, by all accounts, your father is ill. I'm going to see that you reform from now onwards, my lad.'

'My father has been ill for years,' said Raymond sulkily. 'What do you expect me to do — nurse him all day? And why can't Delia leave me alone? I can damn well tell you I'm in a mess now.'

'What do you mean?'

'Spider has my I.O.U.'s. They run to thousands, and he accepted them because he knows I can get the money from my father. But I want to win the money. Now you've spoilt it.'

'Just let Spider try to get cash for his I.O.U.'s and he'll find I'm in the way,' said Tim Ryan.

'Are you going to keep me locked up?' sneered the other. 'Because I can tell you I won't allow you or anyone else to order me around.'

'Meaning you'll pop back to Spider's exquisite company?' snapped Ryan.

'I tell you I've got to!' There was wildness in Raymond Lucas's voice. 'There are other things. Things you wouldn't know about.'

'I know a little bit about everything,' said Tim Ryan. 'For your information,

I'm a private investigator and one of the most highly paid in London. That means I've got to know a lot. What have you been up to in Spider's unsavoury circle?'

'Look!' Raymond said. 'If it's money you're after — I suppose Delia is paying pretty strongly — I'll give you money to leave me alone. I'll be all right. I can work everything out.'

His tone was urgent and scared.

'You'll work out in the assizes some-day,' said Ryan. 'Now I'm going to help you quit playing the fool. You're going with me, and not back to your Bayswater home.'

Ryan hailed another taxi.

Some fifteen minutes later Tim Ryan was standing at the main entrance to a sombre stone building. He had just rung the bell. At the roadside a taxi was waiting, while the driver watched curiously as Ryan struggled with Raymond Lucas. The younger man was no stronger than a woman and a great deal softer than some. Ryan held him by one hand, using a wrestling grip that frequently caused the other to cry out with pain.

'If you had any sense, you'd stop fighting,' said Ryan grimly. 'Now this building belongs to a friend of mine. It's a private mental home, and what goes on in here is nobody's business. You'll stay here until further orders, and they depend on you seeing sense. Tomorrow I'll have a talk about you with Delia.'

The door opened and a large man stood framed in a bluish light. Ryan propelled the Lucas boy into the square hall.

'Hello, Mellick. I want you to look after this chap for a few days.'

Hubert Mellick, whose official qualifications were obscure but whose knowledge of human nature was great, led them silently to an adjoining room.

'I'd like to talk to this young man alone for five minutes, Mellick,' said Ryan, and the large man withdrew. Ryan gripped Raymond's arm again. 'Now out with it! What mix-up have you got into with Spider Malan?'

'I won't tell you!' gasped the other. 'I can see you're an unscrupulous swine, Ryan. You can't keep me here. It's illegal detention.'

'Perhaps, but it will do you good and save you — or your father — some money. Now don't be a fool! Can't you see I'm trying to help you? I can assure you Delia is not paying me any money — though Mellick will require payment. Now you have something on your mind apart from those I.O.U.'s to Spider: What is it?'

'I'm hanged if I'll tell, you. It's my business. You'd only get me into worse trouble. I'll get out of here, Ryan.'

He had the sulky defiance of a cornered weakling. He was like a small mongrel dog yapping his defiance until someone raises a foot.

Ryan nearly hit him, but he controlled his temper. He went to the door and called for Mellick.

'Put him somewhere secure, Mellick,' said Ryan. 'I'll be up tomorrow. He's a young fool who needs protection from himself.'

Tim Ryan went back to his flat that night after 'phoning Delia and telling her just enough to set her mind at rest. Tactfully, he didn't tell her that her brother was in a mental home. That could come later. He promised to meet Delia early next morning.

★　★　★

Ryan was punctual and was surprised to find Delia Lucas waiting for him in the vestibule of the block. She was dressed smartly in a black morning outfit with a chic hat perched impudently on her golden hair. She spoke breathlessly.

'Take me to Raymond, please!'

Mellick's establishment lay along the Harrow Road and the grounds of the small, gaunt building backed on to a canal. Within ten minutes of crawling through traffic-crammed streets, Ryan pulled up at the place. A nurse opened the door to his ring, and they went inside.

'What sort of place is this?' asked Delia. Her eyes crinkled up to his in an inquiry.

'It is a mental home, and the proprietor is a friend of mine,' said Ryan uncompromisingly. 'I can think of no other safer place for Raymond except a police cell

172

and that's where he'll end up if we aren't careful. Let's go to him.'

Raymond Lucas was sitting disconsolately in a strong room, which, without the bed and chair, was more or less a cell. The small window was barred, and the room was on a second floor. The building was old and made of thick stone,

Delia went to him and hugged him. Raymond, to cover his humiliation, turned on Ryan in anger.

'You swine! This place is a lunatic asylum. Let me out!'

'He intends to go straight back to Spider and his friends,' stated Ryan. 'I leave it to you, Delia. What shall we do with him? I think he's mixed up with Spider or some of his pals to greater extent than gambling debts, but he won't talk.'

'Raymond, please let us help you!' Delia pleaded.

Guilty shame and anger struggled together on the young man's face. He turned fiercely on Ryan as if he was the cause of all his troubles, and then snapped at his sister:

'If you must know, I'm in a cursed mess, but I'm not telling this snoop anything. Delia, I want you to get me out of here. Go to the police — anything!'

'Will you give me your word of honour you'll not go back to Spider Malan?' asked Delia gently.

He twisted his lips in humiliation. He was not too far gone to retain some sense of personal honour. He knew he could not descend to making a vow with his own sister, and then violating it. In anger and self-pity, he whined:

'I can't do that!'

Delia was determined.

'I must have your word, Raymond, before you leave this place.' Her eyes sought Ryan's instinctively, and he nodded reassuringly.

'I'll leave you two for a few minutes,' said Ryan grimly. 'If you've any sense, Raymond, you'll let us help you.'

'You can go to the devil!' was the hysterical retort.

Tim Ryan went outside into a hall. He sat on a hard cane seat and lit a cigarette. He sat thinking furiously for five minutes, wondering what other trouble clung to the young idiot. It seemed incredible that a splendid girl like Delia should have a waster for a brother.

Suddenly the door opened and Delia came out.

'Take me back home, Tim,' she said. 'Raymond will have to stay here.' She was white-faced. She did not meet Ryan's eyes

'What is wrong?' he demanded.

'Wrong? Nothing — I — I want to go home to think. Raymond will not give me his word. He'll have to stay here where he's safe. He is safe here, Tim, isn't he?'

As Ryan nodded, Delia's brain reeled with the ghastly things Raymond had told her and the horrible task that faced her.

4

Streets of Soho

When Delia insisted on going straight home without making any definite date for the next meeting, Tim Ryan knew at once that something Raymond had said had upset her. He made a judicious attempt to pick her thoughts, but she evaded the issue.

As they climbed from his car, he asked bluntly:

'What are you going to do about your brother?'

'Leave him where he is for a few days,' she said swiftly. For a moment a softer look came into her eyes. 'You've been very kind, Tim. I won't forget it.'

'Can't I see you again today?'

'No. I — I have things to do, Tim,'

'I'll 'phone you tomorrow morning early.'

'But not too early I hope!' She laughed

and ran up the steps.

Back in his car, Ryan wondered if he should go back to Raymond Lucas and force some explanation from that young wastrel. But he returned reluctantly to his office in Baker Street. It had occurred to him that Delia might be more than annoyed if she learned how he had got tough with her precious brother.

Meanwhile, Delia sat in her room for the next hour thinking furiously of Raymond's desperate request. Then she came to a decision. Her mind was made up.

That night she rang up Peter Arnell and asked him to come over — within the hour if he could. Then Delia dressed carefully in an emerald evening dress and withdrew a short mink coat from a wardrobe.

Just before Peter Arnell called with a taxi, Delia scanned her cheque book and placed it in her evening handbag.

Fifty minutes after ringing Peter Arnell she was sitting with him inside a taxi while they sped to Soho.

'I want you to take me to Nick Casey's place, Peter.'

His dark eyes showed astonishment.

'But that's an awful dump in Soho!'

'I know. That's where we are going, isn't it?'

'But Delia, darling, I thought we might dine somewhere decent.' He was shrewd enough to see the trouble in her blue eyes.

'I have to see someone in Nick Casey's,' she insisted.

'A man?'

'No — a woman,' she said curtly.

Peter Arnell tried to infuse reproach into his tones, and, because he was a born actor, succeeded.

'Heavens! I thought we were to be alone tonight, Delia darling!'

'I shall see this woman only for a little time,' she said sharply. 'It's — a — a matter of business.'

Delia had thought it wiser to go accompanied by a male escort after her nightmarish experience at Cellini's, and she might have enlisted Tim Ryan's aid had not Raymond been so bitterly prejudiced against him. Desperately Raymond had asked Delia to help him — on condition that she promised not to tell Ryan anything. In Raymond Lucas's bigoted mind, Ryan was undoubtedly connected with the police. Delia, anxious to help her brother out of his troubles to a straight and decent life, had agreed to keep Raymond's secret.

Inside the nightclub she looked round for the woman Raymond had described. It was not difficult to recognise her, and as Delia sat down at the table with Peter Arnell, she wondered about ways and means of approaching the woman. After Peter ordered wine, Delia sat playing with the stem of the glass and carefully watching the woman.

Gloria Campton belonged to a gad-about section of the class who had money, education and breeding. Gloria and her set consistently abused all three attributes in order to live faster than nature intended. In appearance she was well-groomed, with raven black hair which flowed down her neck in similar style to that of a famous film actress. But to Delia the woman bore unmistakable signs of the life she was living.

This was Raymond's friend! And Raymond, her brother, was little better than she! Gloria Campton was a cocaine addict, as Raymond had said, and if the woman was just a fool, then Raymond and Spider Malan and his associates were worse.

Suddenly the woman rose and made towards a passage, which led, Delia knew, to a ladies' cloakroom.

'That's the woman I want to see, Peter,' Delia murmured and rose. Peter Arnell showed his astonishment.

'Heavens, Delia. Is that creature a friend of yours?'

Murmuring an apology to Peter, Delia followed the other woman and caught up with her in the passage.

'Excuse me. You're Gloria Campton, aren't you?'

The woman turned swiftly, giving a suspicious look.

'You haven't met me,' went on Delia quietly, 'but I'm Raymond Lucas's sister. I'm Delia. I want to talk to you.'

'What about?' asked the woman harshly.

'Let's go over to this small lounge,' said

Delia. 'Raymond sent me.'

They sat down in the quiet lounge; away from the main hall and dance floor. Gloria ordered two drinks from a passing waiter.

'Raymond owes you some money,' said Delia. 'Doesn't he?'

Gloria Campton narrowed her dark eyes, ignoring the question.

'Why isn't he here? He arranged to meet me.'

'He can't be here. And I know why you arranged to meet, so you can speak out. Raymond won't bring you any more drugs.'

'What's wrong with him? Is he playing the dirty on me?' demanded the woman fiercely.

Delia tried to be patient, hiding her aversion.

'I tell you my brother is finished with the horrible business. Now you gave him £500 to buy drugs from a man called Spider Malan. Raymond was a sort of agent. He told me nearly everything! He's finished and I want to pay you back your money. I'll write you a cheque.'

'I don't want the money!' blazed Gloria. 'I want the stuff. If Raymond doesn't get the stuff, I'll make him suffer. The police will find out just exactly what he has been doing lately.'

Delia could have slapped the woman's hard, painted face.

'Raymond told me you were vicious and would land him in a ghastly mess if he didn't get the drugs for you, but you'll have to see sense,' Delia said tensely. 'Raymond sent me to try to make you accept a cheque. After all, surely you can obtain your drugs from someone else?'

'What do you know about it, you little fool!' cried Gloria Campton furiously. 'How much stuff do you imagine £500 can buy? Quite a bit, let me tell you, and it is for some friends of mine. Perhaps Raymond told you about our club?' She was sneering now. 'Or did he?'

'He said you were the leader of a club of dope addicts,' said Delia sharply.

'Thanks. As a matter of fact, there are nearly fifty of us, and you'd be surprised to hear some of their illustrious names! They are depending upon me, just as I depend on your precious brother. I can't take your cheque.'

'Why not?' asked Delia desperately.

'Because I have to answer to so many others. They'd kick up a row, and anything might happen. Where's Raymond? Has he left Spider Malan?'

'Yes. He's through with the filthy game!' Delia retorted angrily. 'Why, don't you go to Spider Malan's headquarters and get the beastly stuff yourself?'

Gloria said nastily: 'Look here, this is my limit. Nick's place is fairly respectable. Spider hangs out at Charlotte Hi's place. He is hardly seen moving about in daylight. Let me tell you, my child, that women have gone into Charlotte's place and never been seen again, What do you imagine could happen to me walking into that hole with £500? Some might risk it, but I won't.'

'Then you won't let me pay back the money Raymond owes you?' said Delia helplessly.

'You can go back to Raymond and tell him to stop acting the fool,' snapped Gloria. 'Tell him to come here before

Nick closes, and tell him to bring the stuff.'

'And what if he doesn't?'

Gloria raised her cigarette with shaky hand and gulped a lungful of smoke before replying.

'The police need only an anonymous note to set them on the track of anyone suspected of dope-peddling. I could send that note without any danger to myself, I could give the name and address of one or two other people — outside my set — who are expecting Raymond to call on them during the next few days. If the police called instead, these people might become frightened and blab. Now Raymond knows this. He ought to know he can't get away with letting us down.'

'You're bluffing!' said Delia scathingly. 'My brother is a scared idiot to allow you to bluff him. Well, you can't bluff me.'

The other woman twisted her mouth.

'You utter fool! I'm not bluffing. What on earth is wrong with Raymond? Why can't he get the stuff? It's pretty simple. After all, he makes something on the game, and runs little risk. Now he is upsetting the whole show and stirring trouble for himself.'

Delia rose.

'I'll offer you my cheque for the last time. I'm not impressed by your bluff. If that's all it amounts to, we'll risk it. One thing is certain — Raymond won't call on anyone in the next few days if I can help it.'

Gloria smiled, showing her teeth.

'So he's hiding? I always knew he was a weak-kneed fool.' She stubbed out her cigarette desperately. 'Give me the cheque. I'll have to get the stuff somewhere else.'

Delia sat down quickly and wrote out the little pink slip. She ripped out two slips and wrote on the back of one: 'I, Gloria Campton, agree not to threaten Raymond Lucas in future. I admit I am equally involved in the drug traffic.'

'If you sign this,' said Delia calmly, 'I'll give you the cheque. Otherwise I might be inclined to tell you to bung your anonymous notes to anyone you like and keep my money. I'm calling your bluff now, Gloria.'

Delia felt that she had successfully got

the better of the other woman.

Raymond was weak. He had been so scared that this woman would give him away somehow that he had been terrified when Tim Ryan put him inside the mental home.

'I'll sign,' said Gloria. Her voice became whining. 'He's let me down, the fool! He's let me down! What else can I do?'

As Delia came into the restaurant and made her way towards Peter Arnell, Nick Casey murmured to his companion, a little man who was standing with the nightclub proprietor beside the noisy band.

'That's the Lucas girl, Sid. She was in here last night with Ryan.'

'Don't we know it,' lipped Sid Simake. 'Spider would like ter meet the bloke who tipped Ryan off. Well, so long.'

As the little man left, Nick Casey watched him with frozen eyes.

Delia came to Peter's table. He rose and helped her with her chair.

'Are you finished with that ghastly-looking woman, Delia?'

'I wanted to speak to her about an

unfortunate friend,' said Delia. She glanced at Peter. Now that her business at Nick Casey's place was ended she wondered why she had not asked Tim Ryan to come along instead of Peter.

Ryan would have dealt even more efficiently with Gloria Campton's threats and it could have been arranged so that Raymond never knew Ryan had interfered, even if this meant going back on her word to her brother.

'What about another drink?' Peter asked.

'I could do with something strong,' admitted Delia. 'Then we might dash off somewhere else where we can do something in peace.'

Peter tried to get a taxi, but none seemed to be near. They walked along the pavement of the ill-lit street.

'Dashed morbid place!' said Peter uneasily. If his muttered words had been a signal, they could not have been more applicable. From out of the shelter of a gloomy doorway, which they had just passed, three men leaped on them.

Round the corner, in an incredibly narrow alley, stood a car, and a driver revved the engine.

As the attacking man clutched at Peter Arnell and Delia, a dark figure of a man seemed to leap along the street and hurl himself into the fray. To any passerby the scene would represent the not uncommon spectacle of a street fight in Soho — with the inevitable woman, too!

But to Tim Ryan, who had followed Peter Arnell and the girl patiently all night, the attack represented something he had anticipated ever since Delia had left Raymond with the obvious intention of again wandering into risky territory.

He had intended to keep an eye on her for safety, and this was the result.

Peter Arnell had staggered back in astonishment. A lean individual sent him sprawling with a nasty uppercut. Ryan butted in at this juncture, taking the unfortunate film star's place. The lean one received a wicked punch right between his eyes, which brought coloured lights stabbing through his brain. Another blow followed rapidly and the man buckled up. Ryan turned to a smaller man whom he recognised as Sid Simake. One blow sufficed for the Soho rat. Delia fought wildly, with all the vigour of her temper and youth, but the tables turned when Ryan grabbed her attacker by the collar and heaved him against the wall. The man yelled with pain as rough brick afforded no soft bed, and then he tried to use his knuckle-duster while Ryan closed in for the knockout.

Ryan saw the horrible weapon glint dully, and, matching foul play with the only alternative, kicked at the other's shins. As the man howled with pain, his arm lost its momentum, and Ryan swung two smashing blows to the mouth. The man sagged against the wall.

Delia turned and ran to Tim Ryan. The car in the alley growled, and the driver backed recklessly into the grim shadows. Peter Arnell climbed unsteadily to his feet.

Ryan held Delia tightly.

'I knew you were going to walk into trouble, Delia. So I — I followed.'

'I'm glad you did.'

Suddenly she heard Peter Arnell's plaintive voice.

'I say, what a ghastly street! Attacked by a gang! Incredible!'

'Some of Spider's men,' commented Ryan. He was still holding Delia, wondering if her thoughts were identical with his. He was wishing that Peter Arnell would run away and hide.

'I suppose they're after Raymond,' said Delia.

Ryan nodded.

'They might think they can get him back through kidnapping you. Apparently Spider would like to keep his prize sucker and hopes to get cash for his I.O.U.'s.'

'That means they know Raymond has not gone back home to live in a normal manner,' said Delia quickly.

'Spider would soon learn that. He would soon know that I was with you in Nick Casey's place last night. I only hope Nick does not get in bad with Spider. That rat could wreck any place.'

Tim Ryan escorted Delia down the street until they came to a broader, well-illuminated street. Peter Arnell followed, gloomily holding his chin. At the dark corner three thugs stirred and got unsteadily to their feet. They did not know, though they might have suspected it, that they had just encountered one of the hardest-hitting men in London.

At the taxi stand Peter held out his hand to Ryan.

'I say, we're awfully glad you happened to come along. Good show!'

Ryan had to hide a grin at the other's blindness.

'The truth is — ' he began.

'Peter you idiot, this is Mr. Tim Ryan, a private investigator. It wasn't exactly by chance he came along. Mr. Ryan is helping me. That attack was deliberate.'

'Oh, was it?' Peter Arnell gasped. 'But, Delia, why should anyone attack you? Have you been making enemies?'

Delia frowned. She felt reluctant to tell him all about Raymond. Somehow she felt that Peter Arnell would not quite understand.

'Yes, I have enemies,' she said slowly.

'And you knew you'd be in danger tonight!' He was horrified.

'Well, I didn't think about it. I came to see a woman.'

'But those awful thugs! Did you see one had a knuckle-duster? Good heavens Delia — a blow across the face with one of those — ' Peter's hand shot to his face. 'It would leave a ghastly mark. Delia; you mustn't come into this quarter again!'

'What if I wanted to come down tomorrow night?' she asked slowly.

'But you mustn't! I — I couldn't — you must go to the police.'

'I know you couldn't risk your valuable beauty,' she retorted. 'Good night, Peter. We weren't officially engaged, so I haven't a ring to give you. And I don't need the police. I know someone better.'

5

Fallen Too Far

'Weren't you a little hard on Peter?' asked Ryan as they sat back in a taxi which was taking Delia home.

She shrugged. 'Perhaps. But he disgusted me with his futile bleating. Anyway, Peter and I have been drifting away from each other for some time.'

Ryan was quite willing to hear the information.

'Now what did Raymond say which made it necessary for you to visit Nick Casey's place?' he began.

She hesitated. 'I shouldn't tell you, because I promised Raymond. But he's so terribly weak, and after tonight I'm sure I need your help.'

'You can rely on that, Delia.'

Delia showed the statement, which Gloria Campton had signed.

'She could, of course, claim that the

signature had been signed under duress,' commented Ryan, 'but I fancy she wouldn't like the police to see this. Good work, Delia.'

The taxi travelled briskly towards Delia's home and occasional lights from the streets flickered across Delia's face. Ryan thought she looked unbearably lovely.

'If Spider wants cash for his I.O.U.s, he might make trouble,' said Ryan thoughtfully. 'Tonight proved that. Hearing about us being in Nick Casey's place proves to him that I'm working for you, and he knows Raymond has not returned to his home to live. So he thought of an obvious stunt: he would snatch you and later I would get a note saying you would be released if Raymond came back to the fold. You're a marked woman, Delia . . . Spider must think a lot of your brother. But maybe it's all a question of money. How much money can Raymond get hold of?'

'Father doesn't grudge him a penny,' said Delia quietly. 'Once Raymond had a job and an allowance. He threw up the position with the export firm and told father that he was going into business on the Stock Exchange and would need money. All lies! He got a fine sum and then started gambling. I suppose one contact led to another until finally he got into Spider's clutches,'

'Couldn't you get his allowance stopped?' queried Ryan.

'Only by telling my father everything about Raymond, and I'd hate to do that whilst dad is so ill. He would worry so much that — well, it might be fatal.'

'That's tough.'

'But if I can persuade Raymond to throw up the whole beastly game then we might move down to Bournemouth. At the moment, however, dad has a fine Harley Street specialist attending him. It is heart trouble and complications. Dad seldom moves from the flat now.'

'You've got a whole heap of trouble,' said Ryan. 'Spider Malan's got you down on his list, but I'm not going to let them get you.'

He put his arm on her shoulder impulsively. Then he was about to draw his arm away, realizing she had troubles enough without his adding to them, when she suddenly leaned close to him. Her hair was sweet against his face. He caught the fragrance of some perfume she used. His heart raced like a youth who was in love for the first time.

★   ★   ★

The next morning Delia went to see her father as she usually did when he was having his invalid breakfast. He smiled up at her from the bed — a pale man with iron-grey hair and dignified features. Obviously Delia and Raymond had inherited their good looks largely from their thorough-bred father, though Delia's mother, when she was alive, had been a beauty in her day.

'Feeling better today, Daddy?'

He smiled.

'I do feel a little better. Have you heard from Raymond yet? But perhaps he is travelling on business, as he told me he would be.'

'Oh, Raymond will be round before

long,' she said casually.

She straightened his bed and brought him the *Times*. She stayed until the nurse got Mr. Lucas into an invalid chair and wheeled him to the small study, which had been his delightful retreat in more active days. Here Mr. Lucas could look down at the passing crowds in Bayswater Road.

After Delia left, because she had arranged to go with Tim Ryan to see Raymond at Hubert Mellick's mental home, a man and a woman, sitting inside a car in a parking place near the block of flats watched her interestedly.

'She's going for a taxi,' said the black-jowled man whose name was Spider Malan. His eyes were grim and sombre. He did not like leaving his Soho haunts in daylight. 'Now what? Is she going any place in particular?'

'She might be going to see that private detective you told me about,' said Gloria Campton.

Gloria had seen the fight with Spider Malan's three Soho rats last night and, greatly daring, had talked to Sid Simake.

She had learned that Spider wanted Raymond Lucas in order to press for payment of the I.O.U.'s. Gloria had told Sid that she would like to help Spider get even with Raymond or Delia, but Spider would have to come to Nick Casey's faintly-respectable joint. Spider had made the trip and they had talked. Gloria wanted revenge, even if she could not write her anonymous letter to the police.

'We'll split,' said Spider Malan. 'I'll take a chance on that skirt not being out for a pleasure trip. She might be going to see her stinking brother. I want that guy. He's too rich a mug to lose.'

'And what do I do?' inquired Gloria Campton.

She sat next to a man who was a callous rat without scruple, and she had had every social advantage. She had fallen too far for her latest exploit to cause her any dismay.

Spider opened the car door:

'You get out,' he said curtly, 'and if you want to spill the beans to the old man, now's your chance, if you can get in. I'm trailing that dame.'

Gloria Campton curled her lip. She climbed from the car and a second or two later Spider Malan drove into the main road, watching Delia as she boarded a taxi not far distant.

Gloria Campton hesitated, and then walked across the road. She approached the main entrance to the block of flats, walking along the curving path.

Five minutes later she was successfully pretending to be an old friend of Delia Lucas to the maid who answered the door.

6

Gang Warfare

It was a curious sidelight on Raymond's character that he did not regard himself as a weak fool. He had been unlucky. He had mixed with some queer people, but what did that matter? He was over twenty-one and was his own master.

Anyway he would get out of this prison-like place. Only that morning he had given a note to the half-witted man who brought his breakfast. The man had seemed to understand. Raymond had quickly impressed upon him that he would give him some money if the note were handed to one of the tradesmen who called. The note was folded and stamped, and if the tradesman would post it, Spider Malan would indeed receive an interesting communication.

That was why he had refused to commit himself to Delia. He had other schemes.

But Raymond did not know that the note would get no further than Mellick, who read it with an amused smile.

Meanwhile, Delia went indoors, flung off her coat impetuously and ran to her father's study. She paused when she saw the room was empty and then walked. quickly to his bedroom.

Nurse Talbot was attending to Mr. Lucas and the Harley Street specialist, Doctor Garner, was scribbling rapidly in his notebook. As Delia entered swiftly, the tubby Doctor Garner took her to one side and whispered:

'Your father has had a serious relapse. I was hoping his recent improvement was permanent . . . I did not expect this.'

Delia's spirits sank. Doctor Garner's voice was sombre, hinting at more than his words conveyed. Delia came to the bedside and looked down at her father with a sudden fear tugging at her heart.

Mr. Lucas was semi-conscious. His white face matched the pillow, except for the bluish tinge on his lips. He did not know Delia was present. He did not stir.

Nurse Talbot spoke in a husky whisper

and her words were grim.

'He was splendid until that woman wormed her way past the maid. I happened to be making some tea for Mr. Lucas, and when I came back that woman was talking to him. He waved me away, but I noticed he was losing strength with every word she uttered!'

'But dad receives no one except old friends,' said Delia. 'Who was this woman?'

Within half a minute Nurse Talbot had described Gloria Campton, and Delia understood everything. Gloria, wanting to get her own back on Raymond and perhaps on Delia, too, had told an ill man the worst news any man could receive regarding his only son. The result was that Mr. Lucas had collapsed.

Delia tightened her fists furiously. If her father did not recover, Gloria Campton was practically a murderess. The woman had known, probably from Raymond's earlier talks, that Mr. Lucas was a sick man.

For the next hour Delia sat in the bedroom, numb with worry. She forgot all about Tim Ryan and Raymond and the events of the past few days, and all her thoughts concentrated upon the sick man she loved — her father. She was a girl and yet a woman, too, and she gave her silent devotion to praying that her father might recover. Hour after hour, all through the anxious afternoon, she sat watching him. There seemed little else to do despite her anxiety to help in every way. There was nothing to do but wait until the sick man showed some sign of returning from his coma, and then speak encouragingly to him.

Delia moved only once from the bedroom. She telephoned Tim Ryan and told him everything.

'Please, Tim, go over for Raymond. He must be here in — in — case — anything happens.'

'I'll go over immediately, Delia,' he promised. 'I'll bring him back.'

And so Raymond Lucas returned to the block of flats, and Spider Malan, busy contacting a motley crew of thugs and gangsters in Soho, never knew about it.

Raymond came into the room in which

his father lay, and his face was haggard and white. Tim Ryan waited in an adjoining lounge, smoking tensely.

'Delia — I — I don't know what to say!' Raymond's voice was hoarse. Sweat glistened on his brow. 'Ryan had told me about the swinish Campton woman. I could kill her!'

Doctor Garner held up his hand for silence.

'I think I may safely say Mr. Lucas is recovering,' he said slowly. 'His pulse is beating more strongly.'

Within a few minutes Mr. Lucas opened his eyes, uncomprehendingly at first and then with a light of recognition as he saw Raymond.

The young man advanced. Raymond realised with a clarity he had never known before how much he was responsible for his father's relapse. If he had not acted like a callous swine, Gloria Campton could not have struck at him through his father.

The revelation was like a hammer crashing at his innermost thoughts, He fell to his knees before the bed and put his arms round his father.

Delia came out to Tim Ryan and, awkwardly, he offered her a cigarette.

They were smoking silently in the lounge when Raymond came along.

'You'll have no more trouble with me,' he said chokingly. 'I think you can see Dad now, Delia.'

She slipped away quietly, and Raymond stared haggardly at Tim Ryan.

'I know you think I'm an utter fool, and I suppose I am. Well, you can say what you like. You've been helping Delia, I know.'

'I tried to,' said Ryan.

'I'll have to keep out of the way of Spider Malan,' said Raymond nervously.

'He's a dangerous man,' warned Ryan. 'But he can't legally press for settlement of gambling debts.'

'He'll be furious that I'm finished with him.' Raymond straightened his back, squaring his shoulders. When he lost his slight slouch, he was nearly an inch taller than Tim Ryan. 'I think I've come to my senses, Ryan. I told Delia I could win the money again, but now that Dad knows the truth about everything, it would kill him if I went on.'

'You can't win playing against Spider,' stated Ryan.

Raymond nodded uncertainly.

'Well, I'm through! Definitely through,' he said emphatically, as if trying to convince himself.

'I'm glad to hear it,' said Tim Ryan, and he offered him a cigarette. 'Cheer up, old lad. We'll soon get everything straightened out.'

★　★　★

That night two carloads of thugs and Soho ruffians left Charlotte Hi's grimy premises where they had gathered at Spider's invitation. As well as the driver in the leading car sat Spider Malan, and in the rear seat were three thugs of varied ugliness. They had only one thing in common and that was their unsavoury appearance and the guns in their pockets. These men were the new type of underworld rat and they carried weapons. As of old, the favourite device for a fight in which silence was needed was the knuckle-duster and a knowledge of every foul trick possible, but even the knuckle-duster had evolved during the years. Now it was simplicity itself. It was simply a rolled-up newspaper gripped in the fist with three pennies wedged in the three spaces of the four fingers. The pennies protruded, their bases resting against the roll of paper.

A blow with this weapon could rip a mouth or nose in terrible fashion, and, what was important, if dropped it could not be identified. The old knuckleduster, being an individually-designed weapon, did not possess this advantage.

Spider's car led the way to the Harrow Road. They were on their way to snatch Raymond Lucas from Mellick's home. It had not taken any great effort of intelligence on Spider's part to deduce that Raymond was quartered in the home.

The two cars purred along the road, mingling with the general flow of evening traffic that poured through the arteries of the city. Within a short time the cars came to Mellick's stone establishment. They did not draw up outside the door, but parked a hundred yards from the main entrance.

Of the ten men who got out of the cars, four walked down the cul-de-sac and promptly climbed the wall. Being accustomed to this sort of thing they were over in a few seconds, and they dropped lightly on to the lawns inside the home. Spider Malan led his men up to the main entrance, which was approached by a flight of steps from the street. They moved silently, and he knocked on the door discreetly, while three of his men looked up and down the thoroughfare. They were looking for anything that resembled the shadow of a leisurely walking policeman.

Their boldness proved better than caution, for long before any policeman appeared, the door to the home opened. Mellick's matron, clad in spotless uniform, had answered the knocking.

'Step aside, sister!' snarled Spider, and he lunged forward, gripping the astonished woman and clamping an unclean hand over her mouth. The other men poured in after him and closed the door.

They were rats of the night, gangsters and murderers. They knew their onions. One stood by the door whilst others ran into the corridors of the rambling old place.

'Where's Raymond Lucas kept?' snarled Spider, and he eased his hand from the matron's mouth. For answer she attempted to scream, and Spider clamped his hand down again viciously.

Hubert Mellick heard a sound as one of Spider's men blundered against a hallstand, and he looked out of his office door. One quick glance sufficed for Mellick, and he darted into his office again. He shut the thick, solid door and locked himself inside. One of Spider's men thudded against the massive oak-panelled door, and Hubert Mellick went to the telephone.

His quick brain had grasped the meaning of the raid. His first impulse was to dial Tim Ryan's number. Luckily he was through in seconds.

Ryan was resting in his flat. His voice

jerked into urgency.

'It's Spider Malan and his rats. He's dangerous. You want 999, Mellick! The men are killers. Watch out for — '

At that moment the line went dead. One of Spider's men had found the cable and cut it. Spider's voice reached Hubert Mellick through the door.

'Say, you in there! Where's the Lucas mug? I want him. D'you hear? I want him quick.'

Mellick had dealt with criminal types before. 'You're wasting your time. He's not here. He was taken away five or six hours ago.'

'Don't give me that line!' snapped Spider. 'I know he's in this dump. I want him. That boy owes me money, and I want him under my protection.' He gave a guffawing laugh. 'I like the lad.'

'I've phoned the police,' declared Mellick calmly. 'You can argue with them.'

Spider cursed foully. 'I'm sending my men through the wards,' barked Spider. 'You're kidding, I guess.'

'I can assure you I'm not,' said Mellick,

but it seemed that the other had walked away for there was no reply.

Hubert Mellick listened carefully, but even the sounds of the commotion the gangsters must have caused in the wards and private rooms did not reach his ears through the solid stone of the building. Five minutes must have passed, and then once more he heard Spider's voice:

'Listen, feller, that boy's not to be found: Where the blazes is he?'

'I've already told you. You are wasting your time. The police will — '

'Forget it!' snarled Malan. 'The police would have got here in two minutes. You're bluffing.'

Mellick heard a growl of voices. Apparently Spider's men had collected round the office door. A heavy object attacked the panels, but did little more than shake the frame. Mellick felt glad he always took care that axes and other weapons were carefully hidden away in the cellars near the heating system.

Then Mellick heard a voice suggesting that Raymond Lucas was in the room. The general chorus that rose seemed to intimate that the others agreed with this opinion. There were no more words from Spider Malan for a few minutes, and then a barrage of blows fell upon the office door.

Mellick watched calmly and brought his thick cane from his desk. Blow after blow, apparently from an axe, which the raiders had found, shook the heavy door. After a few minutes of savage blows, the inside of the door splintered. It seemed that the gangsters would get in. Mellick wondered how he would be treated. They sounded like enraged thugs with very few scruples. Evidently this sort of outrage was a habit with them.

But, with the suddenness of a curtain rising, shots rang out and yells of alarm sounded from Spider's men. Four shots echoed thunderously through the building. A fierce battle seemed in progress outside.

7

'Get That Girl!'

Tim Ryan had rung 999 immediately he realised Mellick's line had been cut. He backed out his car, an old hat wedged tight on his head and a gun in his buttoned raglan coat. He drove his car fast up the Harrow Road and, within two minutes, met two police cars going in the same direction. He recognised, in one car, beside a load of uniformed constables, the Detective-Inspector of the local division. His name was Linson, and he was a friend of Ryan's.

They swept up to Mellick's establishment, and the police skilfully surrounded the block. Whistles blew, summoning other constables from their beats. Then they attacked the door.

Tim Ryan was one of the first to enter. He realised he'd get no medals for his work, but he was feeling that Spider

Malan and his thugs were menaces that should not be allowed to breathe the same air as decent people.

These men were a few of the type that aimed to turn London and other big cities into hotbeds of vice and crime. They had to be rounded up. It was any citizen's duty to help. Ryan was a special sort of citizen, and, anyway, Mellick had been a good friend to him.

It occurred to Tim Ryan that if only Spider Malan could be rounded up he would receive a long sentence for this attack and so end the troubles of Raymond Lucas — and allow Delia to forget the general beastliness. Delia was a marked woman so long as Spider Malan was at large,

In the square hall a miniature gunfight broke out as Ryan and the police barged in. Spider's men retreated down the long corridor, using their guns on the men they regarded as natural enemies. The police were armed and they replied, shooting only when compelled. The gangsters had turned a corner in the corridor, leaving one man wounded. He crawled to the scanty shelter of a doorway, hugging a leg wound, which spurted blood over the oak blocks.

A dope-filled ruffian was holding the corner, shooting blindly down the hall and showing only his wrist. A bullet pinged wickedly through the air before stabbing into the wall. In the confines of the corridor the explosions were deafening. Somewhere a door opened, and Ryan heard the shrieks of terror-stricken patients who had come to the nursing home as a rest cure for tired nerves!

Ryan was with the police behind the short abuttment of wall that gave on to the corridor. Ryan managed to creep up to the corner while the police debated moving through the grounds. While the police talked in curt sentences. Ryan took a risk. He looked round the wall, waiting with his revolver pointed for the appearance of the lastditch gangster.

In a second the man's hand stabbed round the far corner of the corridor. Before his blind shot could explode from his gun, Ryan took a potshot. His gun barked and simultaneously the gangster's wrist spurted blood and his weapon leaped from his grasp. Ryan jumped forward, down the corridor, the police following.

The gunman, clad in a tightly-belted raincoat, was not quick enough to get away, and he was taken by a policeman. All the fight was out of him now.

Ryan ran quickly down the irregular shaped corridor. It seemed that Spider and his men had successfully got out of the building, and Ryan's impression was corroborated when he ran through an open door into the grounds. He was in time to hear three shots and a cry of pain. The sounds seemed to come from the middle of the thickly-shrubbed grounds. Ryan went ahead, with perhaps a little more caution because of the dark and the possibility that any of the tall laurel bushes might hide one of Spider's men.

He saw two police constables. They had climbed the wall before the main force had shattered the front door lock. Ryan waved, and moved ahead of them. He stepped down a path with a quick, lithe step, and immediately discovered a body.

He gave it a glance, found it was a nondescript person with 'rat' written on his features. The two policemen joined Ryan, and he left them, plunging ahead.

He had a grim desire to put an end to Spider Malan. That would solve a lot of problems. If he could see the thug leader only once, a bullet would be a quick ending for the man and there would be no questions asked.

Tim Ryan came to the end of the grounds just in time to see a number of figures scaling a ten feet high stone wall. Ryan took aim and fired. Crack! The man made no sound, but dropped like a dislodged stone. Ryan fired quickly at another figure perched on the top of the wall. The man seemed to dive forward, out of sight on the other side, but Ryan could not be sure whether he had hit him.

When examined, the man in the grounds was apparently dead. He was a beefy, lumbering specimen and his slowness had been fatal, for Spider Malan's other men had all disappeared over the wall. As Ryan cursorily glanced at him to make sure the body was not

Spider, the police constable caught up with him again.

'Give me a lift, officer,' said Ryan. 'I'd like to see over this wall.'

'There's a canal immediately below,' grunted one constable. 'Watch out.'

They were three well-built constables. Ryan was heaved up in a matter of seconds, and he sat astride the wall. His gun was a searching weapon that pointed quickly at every shadow below. Ryan realised he made a target, but that was a risk he had to take. He glanced down at a dull length of water. It showed no ripples now, but obviously Spider Malan and his followers had swam across and disappeared among the huddle of decrepit buildings on the other side. Ryan listened tensely. No unusual noises came to him through the night air. Reluctantly he clambered down to the policeman below.

'They've given us the slip, but we've got four so far that I know,' he said.

'Not bad.'

Policemen were beating through the shrubs of Mellick's home and another party had searched the building in case some gangster was lying low. Ryan ran into Detective-Inspector Linson and gave his opinion that Spider Malan had escaped with some men to the other side of the canal.

'I'll send a car round to scour the district,' stated the Scotland Yard man.

Tim Ryan sought out Mellick. He wanted to give him a few words of advice.

'The police will need to know just what Spider was after,' he said. 'You'll be quite safe in saying Spider made the mistake of imagining that one of his pals had been dumped here by the magistrates. I would like to keep Raymond Lucas out of this, Mellick.'

The other nodded with a grave smile.

'I know what to say. I'll fix it.'

An hour later six men sat before a huge fire in one of the many basements in Charlotte Hi's place in Chinatown. One man had his jacket half on and his left arm was bandaged with a not-too-clean rag. On a table nearby stood three bottles of whisky and a flagon of rum. The wages of Spider's crime were good things, served, however, a trifle crudely. The basement was distempered a hideous green which had gone streaky, and no less than four doors ran off the room. Only two people knew that a huge cupboard, filling a corner of the cellar, hid another door which led to an old and forgotten drain. The drain, filthy and rat-infested, ran under a good many streets of the peculiar locality. Spider Malan and Charlotte Hi were the two who kept the secret of the drain getaway to themselves. Others could take their chances by choosing the other doors in an emergency.

There had been fifteen minutes of lurid threats of what would happen to Tim Ryan if he came to hand, interposed with vilifications of the entire Metropolitan Police Force. Spider Malan reached out and filled his glass again. He went across to the fire and stood with his back to it. The heat felt good when he remembered his frantic swim across the cold canal.

'That was Ryan,' he said. 'He's a flaming swine an' I'll get him for what he's done.'

The man with the injured arm said: 'I'd

like to see him roasting. Tell me when you get him, Spider.'

The sombre droop of Spider's black jowls did not lift as he gulped whisky.

'I'm getting Ryan. He brought the police, see? That other feller must have got through on that stinking 'phone. Well, I'm getting Ryan — and the Lucas mug. That boy gives tone to my parties and when his old man dies he'll be worth a lot. Well, I'm getting Ryan and the boy. We'll roast Ryan.'

'Get the girl, too,' suggested Sid Simake. 'I think Ryan's interested in that pusher.'

Spider fingered his unshaven chin.

'Why not? Maybe Charlotte would like to see her. That would make Ryan hot. Yeah, we'll get the girl. That'll make Ryan squirm. We'll get her good! Listen — '

Spider began to outline his plans.

Meanwhile, at the Baker Street flat, Tim Ryan parked his car in the mews, and then 'phoned Delia and gave her an account of the affair at Mellick's.

'Spider was after Raymond. Evidently he thinks it worth his while to make the raid, but, of course, that sort of thing is characteristic of these thugs. I don't understand how Spider found Raymond was with Mellick. Anyway, it's just as well that Raymond left earlier. I don't know if Spider knows about Gloria Campton queering his pitch, but that is what it amounts to ... How is your father, Delia?'

'Surprisingly, well,' came Delia's voice. 'Raymond has made a confession of sorts. Dad seems to realise Raymond is going to make a big effort. The Campton woman rubbed everything in, Tim. Oh, I hate that woman!'

'Well, she's got plenty coming to her,' said Ryan. 'Delia, can I see you tomorrow? That is, if your father — '

Her voice was warm yet business-like.

'Attend to your business in the morning, but in the afternoon, darling, perhaps — '

'Perhaps we could see a film,' said Ryan calmly. 'How about it?'

'Fine.'

Then Delia made a provision concerning her father. The cinema trip depended on whether he needed her.

Ryan replaced the telephone, stretched and went into his bathroom. Although tired with reaction from the shooting affray at Mellick's mental home, he took a warm shower. The housekeeper, accustomed to Ryan's irregular hours, was still up and, sitting in his jaunty dressing gown, he ate heartily of the pie she provided.

In the morning he slept late, and was aroused by Miss Hudding 'phoning from his office below.

'You have a visitor, Mr. Ryan,' said his secretary. 'A Mr. John Brown, sir.'

Ryan groaned, replaced the 'phone and hurriedly dressed. He had heard vaguely about Mr. Brown. The man knew criminal law backwards.

Mr. John Brown was a plumpish man with a careful smile. He seemed very respectable in his city morning dress.

Ryan hid a yawn as he said: 'You want to see me, Mr. Brown.'

'Yes, about a peculiar case I have on my hands. It's a matter of incendiarism, which is worrying me. My client would like an investigation by a private person.'

'You actually want me to find out the cause of a fire?' asked Ryan impatiently. 'What's wrong with the police or the insurance inspectors?'

'My client has cause to suspect his partner. The insurance inspectors have given the case a clearing, but my client is not satisfied. Yet he does not want to create an awkward conflict.'

'I'm not so sure — ' began Ryan.

The other interposed: 'We merely require you to pronounce a verdict on your findings. The fire happened two days ago at Dover Street. I can take you to the site and your fee will be fifty guineas. I promise you it won't take up more than half-an-hour of your time.'

Ryan got into his hat and raincoat, which hung permanently in his office. He ran a hand over his chin.

'I'll take it on,' he said.

Mr. Brown had a taxi waiting. As Ryan climbed in, he promised himself a big breakfast later, but not much later because he did not intend to give Mr. Brown's client much time.

The car started, and Mr. Brown made some remarks about the placid morning weather. The taxi travelled briskly down the length of Baker Street, and then Mr. Brown slipped a gun from his pocket and pointed it across the taxi compartment at Ryan.

'I am not Mr. Brown. I'm an out-of-work actor and I'm short of money. Don't move. This gun is loaded.'

But Ryan believed in moving while the opposition talked. He propelled himself from the seat, but he was not quick enough to avoid the stream of sickly liquid, which squirted from the man's gun. The liquid caught Ryan full in the eyes, and in a second he was blinded and choked. He sprawled forward unable to judge or control the impetus of his leap. He did know he collided with the actor but his breathing was painful and every gulp seemed to draw a fiery vacuum into his lungs.

His senses began to slip into a mile deep darkness even though he willed fiercely to cling to the edge of consciousness. Then the effort was too great. A great blot of darkness enveloped him.

The man with the water-gunful of liquid chloroform gasped as fumes swirled into his lungs. He reached desperately for the taxi door just as the driver slowed. 'Mr. Brown' jumped to the pavement, gasped at clear air and, as soon as the nearest passerby approached, got into the taxi again.

'Make it snappy to Charlotte's,' he gasped to the driver. 'This beastly stuff is nearly choking me . . . Never mind him.'

8

Beauty in Danger

The taxi carrying Tim Ryan did not go straight to Charlotte Hi's place. All day police had been seen patrolling the vicinity in pairs and some of the lowly, hard-working inhabitants of London's Chinatown had wondered what was brewing. Policemen had actually entered the insalubrious establishment of Charlotte Hi with a warrant, but they emerged with the grim knowledge that they could not prosecute without evidence. Charlotte Hi, with the cunning of her type, showed them a house that apparently existed solely to provide elementary comforts for doss-house habitués!

The taxi stopped inside the stable yard of an old house, which was surrounded on three sides by taller buildings. Ryan was helped out quickly by the taxi driver. The man with the water-gun hoisted

Ryan to his back and staggered in haste into the house.

There were cellars in the house and the unconscious man was taken down crumbling steps by the now perspiring 'Mr. Brown'. In a gloomy cellar the actor-crook walked unerringly towards a hole in the wall. He lowered Ryan urgently into this black gap, and then jumped down. He was in a smelly tubular passage made of worn bricks. He could barely stand upright, and in this manner walked twenty yards in total darkness. Then at a sharp curve a voice grated unexpectedly:

'Okay. I'll take him now . . . See you later, pal.'

Tim Ryan was handed over to Spider Malan in the depths of a forgotten city drain. Spider stumbled along the route, which he had travelled once or twice, and only anticipation of future, cruel enjoyment with his victim stopped Spider immediately venting his hatred on the man he carried.

★ ★ ★

Raymond Lucas left his family's flat after lunch in order to buy some cigarettes. He turned up the road towards a tobacconist. The fine weather seemed to coincide with the lifting from his heart of a great many burdens. He was determined to steer clear of the evils that had lately enslaved him. His father had passed the crisis and was expected to progress favourably. Obviously his recovery would depend upon his being free from worry regarding his son.

He walked past a car drawn up at the pavement edge when a woman's voice hailed him harshly.

'Raymond Lucas!'

He halted and turned. He saw Gloria Campton's head and shoulders at the wheel of a battered car. She was staring at him grimly.

He stepped to the car with a sudden savage feeling. This woman had nearly killed his father!

'You witch! What the blazes do you want? I'd like to — '

'Get in beside me,' said Gloria Campton calmly. 'I want to talk to you.'

He nearly hauled her from her seat, and then his rage subsided to a dangerous calm. He would look a fool provoking a fight in the street, but all the same he would like to give Gloria Campton a thrashing, woman or not.

'Come on,' urged Gloria. 'It's in your own interests.'

He walked round the car, got in the front seat beside her, telling himself that he was more than a match for her.

'You've got a nerve! Let me tell you you're playing with fire. For two pins I'd half kill you!'

She smiled with dangerous charm.

'Don't talk like that Raymond. I — I want to talk to you seriously.'

'What about?'

'Be patient, my child.'

She let in the clutch and eased the car down the road. They turned a corner into a quieter backwater,

'What game are you playing?' demanded Raymond with a catch in his rising voice. He caught her by the shoulder. He was about to bring his other arm to threaten her when a man rose from the back seat.

He was a small man and his name was Sid Simake. He had been hidden under a pile of travelling rugs, but, even so, Raymond had never looked at the rear seat.

'You really are a trusting fool, Raymond,' Gloria laughed musically.

Sid's hand held a pad, which smelled of sickly chloroform. His hands went round Raymond's mouth, pressing the young man's head back against the seat Raymond's struggles lasted less than fifteen seconds, but they were anxious seconds for the two in the car. Sid Simake's beady eyes jerked from one side of the road to the other, watching for any passerby who happened to glance at the car. Sid intended to ease up if anyone displayed special curiosity. Then when they had passed along the quiet street, he would again clamp the pad over the mouth of the dazed man.

But the tricky seconds passed. Raymond lay motionless, breathing slowly and deeply. Sid Simake dropped back to his rear seat and wiped his monkey-like forehead. Gloria Campton accelerated down the street.

'The boss said we had to persuade him,' growled Sid. 'All right fer him! Persuade that perisher! He was tryin' to do fer you, and would have if I hadn't used the dope.'

'I want to get out of this,' said Gloria Campton bitterly.

'Yus,' sneered Sid. 'Yus, you do. But the boss thought you was the one for the job. If you don't like it, the cops might hear about yer stinking dope club.'

'I'm leaving London the moment I get out of this car,' said Gloria tersely. 'I'm not taking any chances.'

★ ★ ★

When Tim Ryan didn't call at the appointed time for her, Delia set off for his Baker Street office.

'Mr. Ryan left a few hours ago with a Mr. Brown and has not vet returned,' Miss Hudding told her.

'Who's Mr. Brown?' asked Delia.

'An amateur lawyer, I think. Mr. Ryan went out without his breakfast so the housekeeper said.'

Delia frowned and tapped her foot. 'Get Mr. Brown on the 'phone. It's urgent.'

The real Mr. Brown was very definite.

'I've never seen Mr. Ryan today or any day,' he said. 'We have never met, though I have heard of Mr. Ryan. If there is anything I can do — '

Delia said quickly: 'I'm sorry; Mr. Brown. Apparently there is some mistake.'

Miss Hudding was puzzled and alarmed. Actually she found most of Ryan's affairs alarming and slightly incredible.

'I assure you, Miss Lucas, the man's name was Mr. Brown — Mr. John Brown — and Mr. Ryan left with him in a taxi.'

Delia's woman's intuition told her that Tim Ryan was in danger, but she controlled her alarm. Instead she reached for the telephone again and dialled 999 and asked for Detective-Inspector Linson. She remembered Tim Ryan telling her about his friend Linson and his part in the fight at Hubert Mellick's mental home.

Delia was fortunate in finding Linson in his office, and quickly she gave the essential facts.

'Well, Miss Lucas, I know Ryan is a

beggar for finding trouble so I wouldn't worry too much. He'll probably turn up, but in any case I'll send a man over to interview Brown.'

As she hung up, Delia realised that Scotland Yard heard every day about people who disappeared and reappeared in the oddest circumstances. Perhaps Detective-Inspector Linson was right, and Tim would turn up with some queer explanation.

She left Miss Hudding. She felt disappointed, puzzled and every few minutes she experienced a wave of apprehension. Somehow she knew Spider Malan was behind this. Delia returned to her flat. She spent some time with her father and then asked the maid if she had seen Raymond.

Raymond, it appeared, had left the flat, telling his father he would be back after he got some cigarettes.

Delia waited and on impulse went out into the busy street. She turned along the Bayswater Road, towards Paddington Station. She had scarcely left the flat when a taxi pulled up at the kerb beside her. The driver beckoned to her.

'Miss Lucas?' said the man quickly.

Delia nodded.

'I was on my way to pick you up,' continued the driver. 'Mr. Ryan has sent me. He wants you to meet him near Regents Park. I'll take you over, miss.'

Sudden relief flooded Delia. Tim Ryan was not in danger. She had just been imagining things, Tim, apparently, was busy with some case, but he wanted to see her just the same!

She jumped into the taxi, and the driver swung round a side street. Delia lay back, and at once she wondered about the peculiar odour that hung in the air of the taxi. It was a sweet, sickly smell though not strong enough to be objectionable. The taxi ran through many smaller thoroughfares and finally came to the green space of Regent's Park. Here, in a quiet, dignified cul-de-sac off Albany Street a man came round the back of the stationery taxi. He wore a dark, raglan coat and a hat pulled down over his eyes. The man opened the taxi door in a jerky, swift manner and climbed in.

'Hello, Tim — ' she greeted and then broke off-with a scream.

The man wasn't Tim Ryan. She tried to cry out, all her instincts of danger aroused, but he pulled her down from her seat to the taxi floor. Here, hidden by the taxi door, he struggled with her, trying to hold a sickly breathtaking pad to her mouth.

He succeeded after a rough struggle in which Delia fought desperately. The pad, held with cruel pressure to her mouth, sent fumes into her lungs with every gasp she took. Her senses swam and finally everything faded into a dark cloud.

The taxi driver, looking warily right and left, swung his car round and headed back towards the city centre.

9

Thug Torture

In a gloomy cellar at Charlotte Hi's, Spider Malan gloatingly surveyed two of his victims.

Ryan had lain in a drugged sleep for an hour and then recovered to find himself bound hand and feet. The wretched cellar was very warm — there seemed little ventilation and the embers of a fire glowed from an open furnace. He had lain all the morning, after recovering consciousness, while Sid Simake and Spider Malan made mysterious journeys in and out of the four doors leading into the place. Once Charlotte Hi came into the cellar and looked at Ryan with her black, dispassionate eyes. And then to Tim Ryan came the grimmest blow. One of the doors opened and Spider Malan walked in with the unconscious form of Delia Lucas across his shoulders! Tim had cried out, throwing threats at the mob leader. Inwardly he had cursed his own carelessness. Then, an hour later, Delia opened her eyes.

'Tim! Where are we?'

'Spider thinks he has us fixed,' said Ryan quietly.

Spider Malan lit a cigarette at the furnace.

'I'm just wondering what to do with you, Ryan. I've got a man who'd like to break every bone in your body. This feller still has a bullet in his arm from the fight the other night. He's feeling rightly sore.'

'That's his worry!' snapped Ryan.

'Then there's the girl,' went on Spider, 'You know, she's worth money.' Spider laughed, crinkling his black jowls. 'I see that gets you. Ryan.'

Ryan had involuntarily shown his teeth. It was an expression of the murderous feeling he bore against Spider Malan when the rat spoke about Delia.

'Let her go, Spider,' he said thickly. 'You ought to know the police will be here. I have my safeguards. When I don't turn up, my secretary calls the police.'

'Is that so?' Spider walked slowly across the room. He came near to Ryan and kicked him violently. 'Well, I should get busy. Then the cops will find nothing if they get into this cellar. But this cellar ain't easy to find, Ryan. The cops have been inside Charlotte's place this morning.'

Spider walked away, his long arms swinging. 'Watch 'em, Sid,' he said to the little Soho runt who was one of the other three present. 'I've got a pal to see.'

Spider left by a door at the far end from Ryan, and the investigator saw a flight of stairs momentarily before the door shut.

Spider Malan went to a room on a floor above the cellars, but even this floor was partially below ground level. He entered the room and stared at the two men inside.

'He's a bit sick, Spider,' said one man. He looked sneeringly out of his cocaine-hazed eyes at the young man who sat in an old wooden chair. Raymond felt sick and this nausea dimmed his anger at being kidnapped by Spider. He was ill and his fury lay checked.

'Hello Ray,' drawled Spider. 'Have a smoke. You'll feel better. Sorry to treat you like this, but I told Sid he had to talk you over. Sid's a blamed fool.'

He handed Raymond a cigarette. The young man nearly threw it in the other's face when he saw it was that insidious weed, Marihuana. Yet Raymond stopped himself. Somehow he felt it would pay him to deceive Spider Malan.

'Thanks,' he said, and he lit the cigarette from Spider's gold lighter. Soon the acrid smoke hung in the air. 'The old smoke, eh, Spider?'

A grin spread over Spider Malan's face. 'There's a game on tonight. How do you know your luck won't change, Ray? That's why I thought I'd get you away from that trickster, Ryan. He's just a cheap dick.'

'What sort of games have you got, Spider?' asked Raymond.

'I got a roulette wheel fixed up. I got some exciting people coming, too. And there's poker.' Spider winked. 'All behind a wall the cops don't know about.'

'Should be good,' muttered Raymond. 'I'm interested.'

'Sure it's good — and safe. The cops are getting sick of walking along the road. They've got another twenty-three gaming-houses to watch besides a few hundred drinking clubs.'

'Well, I've got a little money,' murmured Raymond. 'I'd like a flutter.'

Spider patted his back.

'That's all right. Your credit is good with me. Anyway, you'll be a rich man some day.'

Raymond nearly showed his fury in his face. He lowered his head quickly and stared at the floor.

'Well, I've got to go,' declared Spider. 'See you tonight, Ray.'

Outside in the passage, Spider's twisted mind reflected that in a few more days with the mug taking cocaine, everything would work out fine. Some day the mug would be rich. Spider meant to share that money.

Raymond stared at the dopey man who sat with him. He wanted to get out of this room. He wondered if he had successfully bluffed Spider. Surely the man did not think he was coming back after all that had happened? But Spider was conceited enough for that.

Raymond stood up. The other man watched him with a silly grin. Raymond rubbed his hands, walking slowly round the grimy room. He came near to the filthy fireplace and grabbed at a loose portion of the iron grate. There was nothing else which would suit his desperate purpose. Raymond lunged towards the man, the iron upraised. The other was too slow to avoid the blow, which cracked his head.

The man sagged. He was unconscious and would be for hours. Raymond searched him, but found no weapon except a knuckle-duster. A moment later Raymond went out into the passage. He was trembling.

'I've got to get out of here quick,' he murmured, peering around him. Charlotte Hi's rabbit warren was a maze. Raymond tensed. The sound of harsh voices made him leap back to the shadows, which lurked round the doorway. He listened intently as two men passed.

'Spider's got a girl and Ryan,' one man

said. 'He's going to brand the girl.'

Raymond tried to clear his dazed brain. So Ryan was a prisoner in this place! And the girl? Could — could she be Delia, his sister? Spider was a cruel swine, especially where women were concerned. The horror of this realisation made Raymond's brain work more rapidly. He clenched his fists, and crept down the passage, stealthily following the two men. He opened a door at the end of the passage and was just in time to see a trapdoor close. After a pause, Raymond moved forward and looked through the trapdoor. From it, a flight of wooden stairs ran down into yet another passage.

Raymond went down the stairs, wondering what chance he had of doing anything effective even if he did find his sister and Ryan. He hesitated.

Perhaps he ought to leave it to the police. Well, he'd have to give a warning anyway, and that would mean getting into the street. He pushed on. At the bottom of the stairs ran a subterranean tunnel. Raymond found a door. He stopped and looked at the chink of light, which showed at the bottom of the door.

Spider considered him a guest. Well, he would act like one. He would walk where he chose. A shadowy scheme of bluff developed in his mind. Raymond tried the handle and opened the door.

Like a camera taking a snapshot, he took in the whole scene within a split second. He saw Ryan being gripped by three thugs. The detective was being propelled towards an open furnace. Perspiration flowed down Ryan's face as he resisted. But the sight that made Raymond really sick with horror was his sister, Delia. Her hands were bound behind her, and she was backing away from Spider Malan who was brandishing a red-hot poker in her face!

Raymond ran into the room.

'Take it easy, Spider,' he gasped. 'I don't want my sister hurt.'

Spider dropped the poker. 'That's O.K., Ray, I was only bluffing. I wouldn't hurt a hair on your sister's head. I was only giving Ryan something to think about so as he'd lay off. He's stuck on your sister.'

Raymond spoke in level tones. A

strange calm had come over him. 'I want my sister set free, Spider.'

'O.K., pal. Anything you say. It was a mistake anyway. I never gave orders for her to be trussed.'

'It was a mistake that oughtn't to have been made, Spider,' said Raymond bitterly. 'I don't know that I can trust you any more.'

'You can always trust me, Ray. I tell you, it was a mistake. The boys forgot what I told them.'

Delia ran to Raymond.

'Raymond! Stop them torturing Tim!'

'Ryan can burn for all I care,' snapped Raymond viciously. 'He's on the cops' side.'

Spider grinned again.

'Sure. Ray's coming back to the parties. He don't like Ryan. Take your sister upstairs, Ray.'

Raymond used one arm to propel Delia into the passage. He did not move from the doorway. His face was white. Delia had given him a numb, scared look.

Raymond's hand went to the light switch and he yelled: 'Now, Ryan!'

The glowing fire gave a devilish atmosphere to the cellar as the light went out. The cellar was big and shadows flickered as Raymond leaped towards Ryan.

Tim Ryan made the effort of his life. At Raymond's unexpected shout, he wrenched his arm free. Ryan's brain had worked while Raymond talked to Spider. He thought he knew the boy better than Spider, and he expected some desperate trick.

Ryan's free arm smashed like a hammer into one of the thug's face. The man reeled. The other two tried to hold a man who had suddenly slipped from his jacket. As Ryan ducked below the ribs of the men, he rammed a stomach with a mule-like punch. He darted from the only man who retained a grasp.

Then Ryan was slogging like a fast-moving machine. His grim eyes kept the whole scene in focus. As a man circled to get closer, Ryan leaped to one side. More than one felt a blow from the hardest hitter in town. Two men staggered to the cellar floor temporarily out of the fight.

Another had to turn to deal with

Raymond. The youngster fought like someone possessed. He kicked savagely and flung his fists in a whirl of inspired animal instinct. Ryan got close to him, and their fighting became more effective. Ryan backed steadily to the door, and twice had to kick out at a man who tried to cut off their way of escape.

At the door, Ryan suddenly pushed Raymond through into the passage. Ryan used his shoulder like a rugger player.

'Get Delia away!' he shouted. 'Quick!'

Ryan rammed a man back to his mates like a thrown chair. Then he sprang backwards in a leap that can only be achieved by training. He pulled the door after him. He watched Raymond take Delia up the distant flight of stairs to the dull glow of light that came through the trapdoor.

Three men were pulling on the door, and Ryan let go suddenly. The men staggered and blundered into the others. Ryan used the precious minute to leap to the wooden stairs. He dashed up through the trapdoor as the first of the men came into the subterranean passage. As Ryan raced into the derelict room, Raymond dropped the heavy trapdoor flap. Then he and Ryan paused to heap some junk on top of the trapdoor before they ran into the passage.

Delia was between Ryan and Raymond with Ryan leading and in a cold, killing mood. They jumped up another flight of stairs, which led into a room. Two men suddenly loomed and tried to stop Ryan. He judged the timing of their attack nicely and the crack of his fists on their jaws sounded like leather being smacked.

It was Ryan's hour. They chose a passage leading from the room, and a wildcat of a woman, crazed with dope, had to be hurled out of their way. Behind her lurched a man, and Ryan dealt with him in brilliant fashion. Under the tempo of Ryan's attack he fell as if pole-axed.

Ryan bore the brunt. It seemed that the men in the cellar had had to seek another exit, and they had not yet appeared.

When Ryan saw daylight through some windows in the bewildering building, he knew he was not far from the street. They had to ascend a rickety staircase, attached crazily to a wall without a banister, and then he saw a door, which led obviously to the street.

As they dashed forward, the door burst open and men poured in.

Ryan grinned in relief. The men were in blue police uniform. Leading was Detective-Inspector Linson. Ryan gripped his arm.

'Get Delia and Raymond to safety. I'll show you the layout.'

Linson nodded and took the two out into the street to a police car.

Tim Ryan raced with the police into the cellar. They found the entrance to the drain. Spider, taking a risk once too often, had tried to gain the floor above the cellars and was cut off by the police. With Sid Simake and others they were rounded up, and Ryan, Raymond and Delia had definite charges to lay against them.

★   ★   ★

Some weeks after Spider Malan and his associates, including Charlotte Hi, had been put behind bars, Tim Ryan married Delia and the best man, naturally, was her brother.

'You know,' said Tim Ryan to Delia, 'this sort of thing might happen again.' They were staying at St. Ives, Cornwall, where it is pretty lonely for anyone except honeymooning couples.

'What happen again, Tim? Falling in love?' Delia lay back on the sand. It was secluded. Surf roared and gulls wheeled with plaintive calls. 'I don't mind . . . so long as it's me you fall in love with.'

He kissed her. She lay utterly content. Tim Ryan pressed her close to him with a rising passion and marvelled at his good luck.

'I could fall in love with you a million times,' he said in a low voice. 'But I've got to warn you, Delia, I'm doomed to mix with criminals — or at least, fight 'em.'

'I'll help you fight them.' She wrestled with him playfully. 'When I'm not fighting you.'

THE END